Up
Mountain
One Time

A RICHARD JACKSON BOOK

Orchard Books

A division of Franklin Watts, Inc.

New York • London

Up Mountain One Time

By Willie Wilson

Pictures by
Karen Bertrand

Orchard Books, 387 Park Avenue South,
New York, New York 10016
Orchard Books Canada, 20 Torbay Road
Markham, Ontario 23P 1G6

Orchard Books is a division of Franklin Watts, Inc.

Manufactured in the United States of America
Book design by Mina Greenstein
10 9 8 7 6 5 4 3 2 1
The text of this book is set in 12 pt. Galliard.
The illustrations are charcoal and ink

Library of Congress Cataloging-in-Publication Data
Wilson, Willie. Up mountain one time.
Summary: A mongoose on the Caribbean island of St.
Thomas undertakes a journey from his birthplace in a village
churchyard to his destiny in the bush of the northern
mountains to live wild like his ancestors.
[1. Mongooses—Fiction.   2. Saint Thomas (V.I.)—
Fiction.   3. Animals—Fiction]   I. Bertrand, Karen, ill.
II. Title. PZ7.W69954Up 1987 [Fic] 87-7624
ISBN 0-531-05725-9   ISBN 0-531-08325-X (lib. bdg.)

For Our Parents
Hack and Sallie Wilson
and
John and Annabel Bertrand

A special thanks to
Peter and Isabel

Poncho's Coop

Four Corners

Drake's Seat

Prosper's Place

Manteoba's Tree

Town

The Gut

THE ISLAND

Part One

The Churchyard

One afternoon Viggo sat beneath the calabash tree listening to the goats.

"Today pretty, m'child," one goat said.

"Pretty pretty for true," a second nodded.

"Sunny," said a third.

"Sunny for true."

"The trees them looking well green."

"And the sky looking well blue."

"Blue blue for true."

The goats' talk bored Viggo. He got up and crossed to his perch on the churchyard wall to wait for his mother. He was glad he was a mongoose and not a goat, at least not one tied to a tree. He'd learned from his mother that it was the rope around their necks that made them talk that way.

He looked down at the shantytown street for some sign of her. Shops were closing and night was falling and soon she'd be making her way back home. Each day she left their hill of weeds to scavenge in the streets and gutters below. The street was no place for a mongoose, and it frightened him to know that one day he would have to be brave enough to go there too. But for now his only responsibility was to stay with the goats and avoid getting sat on.

There was still no sign of his mother. Through a patch of banana leaf Viggo spotted a dog ambling toward the garbage bin. Two cats slinked out of it and into the gutter. A third, a thick-headed tom with a torn ear, leaped out and watched the dog from the rim. The dog poked his muzzle into a wet bag and the contents spilled onto the pavement. A door opened and a man yelled and the dog trotted away.

"Cat could jump more than dog," Viggo announced to the wind. "But dog tooth bigger."

His perch gave him a good view of the street from a safe distance, and he was proud of the many things he knew. From his mother he'd learned even of things he couldn't see. Around the bend was the wharf, a place where they cleaned fish. Fish, she informed him, were things that lived in the sea; and the sea, he knew, was the moving blue space between the hills.

A car rattled past the stairwell and sputtered up the street. A new cat appeared below and joined the tom already back on the heap. In the distance, a rooster crowed.

Viggo looked where the sound came from. Above the rooftops, spanning all he could and couldn't see, were the towering green mountains of the north. In these mountains an island mongoose could still find bush. Real bush. His mother promised him that one day, when he was old enough and strong enough and brave enough, they would go there. They would escape garbage and gutters forever to live wild like his ancestors. To prepare him for that day, she told him bush stories and taught him bush things. Viggo learned to yearn for the bush without really understanding what the bush was. He looked at the mountains now, tilting away from him with their dark folds of bush and stone. They seemed far to him and forbidding.

A tin can rolled beneath the stone stairway below him. He heard it hit something, spin, and stop. Then he heard his mother's sounds moving through the dry leaves in the culvert and saw her come out. She carried his dinner in her mouth.

"What that is?" Viggo asked her.

"Chicken wing," she answered wearily. "It have on sauce." She drew close and he smelled a stronger, more pungent odor on her. The scent of an alley cat.

"You had a fight?" he asked her.

His mother nodded.

"The brown?"

"Not he."

"The black and white?"

"A next one," she explained. "A orange fellow living down to the boatyard."

This one was new to Viggo. She bowed her head to show him where the cat had clawed her. The blood matted in her fur gave Viggo a thin, fluttery feeling.

"I give him a good bite," she informed him.

His face squinched up. He couldn't imagine his own mother grappling with an animal as large as a cat. He wanted to know more, to hear for himself how it felt to be locked in combat. Instead, she started an old, less satisfying story that was meant to put him to sleep.

He gnawed the bone, only half listening to the long-ago tale he already knew, about fearless mongooses waging canefield battles with rats. He liked the story of his bush ancestors, but tonight he wanted it to end. The moon was full and the scent of the cat still with him, and he wanted to lie awake with it and puzzle through the business of fighting. He closed his eyes and softened his breathing, pretending to sleep, and before long his mother's story trailed off into silence.

He peeked and saw her rise but not move away. She licked her paw and used it to rub her wound. Then came a bit of chewing and the grooming of coat and tail. When this was done and she was satisfied he was asleep, she went to the far side of the tree.

Later, her friend Clovis came to talk to her. Clovis was the hill's protector, a tough old ramgoat, bearded and weathered, whose neck suffered no rope. When mongrels came to harass the goats, Clovis chased them off. Once Viggo saw him hit a yellow mutt broadside. The butt sent the cur up the steps and through the church door.

His mother talked to the old ram in whispers. Viggo watched their silhouettes, and when he heard Clovis muttering his comforting goat sounds, he guessed they were talking about the fight. He turned his ear out of the wind and inched forward, straining to hear some little thing he wasn't supposed to know. But tonight their whispers were lost to crickets and tree toads.

Soon his mother returned and curled around him. The scent of the cat was still on her, and it stirred the same wonderings it had before. What would it be like to fight a

cat, or worse, a dog? It was one question he hoped never to learn the answer to. He looked at the mountains slanting in the moonglow and, pulling his tail in front of him, he wished his wish—that one day they would go there.

"But not too too soon," he reminded himself in a whisper.

He would go there soon enough, just as soon as he was old enough and strong enough and brave enough to venture beyond the churchyard wall.

A Bush Story

Viggo often talked to himself during the long hours his mother was away searching for food. Usually, he recited the bush stories she told him. As he recited them, he fidgeted with tufts of grass, pulling and picking at them, leaving bald spots as he went along. Most days he could be found beside whichever wall cast the best shadow, mumbling his stories, fumbling with whatever tufts he hadn't already yanked up. It was a lonely occupation.

Telling the stories was part of practicing to be brave. Often other creatures idled by the gate to listen, perhaps a lizard or a tree toad, a bird or maybe two. They seemed to enjoy his chatter. It occurred to Viggo that as a descendant of bush fighters he should be hunting these creatures, not entertaining them. But he enjoyed their company and the hunt was still not in him.

♦

One morning, several days after his mother's fight with the cat, a red wooden pickup truck rumbled into the yard. From the roots of the calabash tree Viggo watched a man untie the goats and one by one move them to another tree. The last was a lame she-goat named Soca. This one the man dragged toward the truck. Soca kicked and butted, and the man groaned and grunted, but he finally wrestled her into the back of the pickup.

The truck started up and banged down the backside of the hill. Her disappearance inspired much chewing and nodding and talk from the others of how lucky she was to be going back to the bush.

"Back to the bush, back to the bush," they baad in unison. "Branga truck gone take Soca back to the bush." This chorus continued for some time, and Viggo wondered why Soca had fought so hard if the man was taking her where she wanted to go.

Later, when he had fallen into one of his stories and was telling it more or less to the view, Clovis came up from behind. The goat waited for Viggo's story to end, but it showed no sign of doing so.

"That's a regular story you telling," he interrupted.

Viggo was startled, embarrassed to be found idling, talking to himself.

"I was just looking to poke a bite in that lizard," he lied, puffing himself up.

"Well, is good you hunting," Clovis said. "Young fellow like you got to be ready for action. In the bush a mongoose your size bringing home dinner already."

"A mongoose could bite hard hard," Viggo announced, making a sure show of his teeth.

"That he can," Clovis agreed.

Viggo was trying to think of another brave remark when bleating erupted by the tree. Two goat ropes were tangled and all the goats were pondering the knots, debating who was at fault. Clovis gave the matter a tired look.

"Why they tie up like that?" Viggo asked.

"The man want them stay one place get fat," Clovis replied without explaining why. Viggo sensed there was a dark side to the business of ropes and making goats fat.

"Clovis?"

"Yes, Viggo."

"If Soca was going back to the bush, why she kick up like she ain want to go?"

Clovis stared at a large stone in the earth as if the answer were buried beneath it.

"Maybe the truck wasn't taking her to the bush," he answered.

Viggo stared at the stone too.

"Where it take her then?"

"Town." Clovis shrugged, looking out across the bay. "Maybe to town."

Viggo looked at this place gleaming like cliffs in the far belly of the harbor, the mountains rising behind.

"And she ain want to go there?" he asked.

"Goats don't like town."

"Why they don't like it?"

Clovis thought a moment and took a deep breath. "Town is a hard place to get back from," he explained. "When a man take a goat town, it ain pasture he going—you could be sure of that."

Viggo was thinking to ask him something else, something more about town, but Clovis turned to go.

"I go leave you get back to your hunting," he said. Viggo watched him walk toward the tree and heard the goats' noise subside as Clovis helped untangle their lines.

That evening, when it was almost time to sleep, Clovis returned. Viggo's mother was telling him the story of his Great Uncle Eno. It wasn't as dark or mysterious as the story about the canefield battles, but he liked it because it told where his mother had migrated from and how she'd been marooned in the churchyard. From where he sat, Viggo could see the dark moonlit land, the very hills Eno and his mother had called home.

"All you had live in the bush?" he asked her.

"Not in the bush bush," she explained. "Eno was too old to hunt, and he use to pick garbage by the barracks yard. We had live in the bushes, yes, but not really in the bush."

Viggo was not clear on what was bush and what was bushes, or where the bushes ended and the bush began. It seemed bush was bushes but bushes not always bush.

"Where we lived was good," her story went on. "The onliest road was a shady lane. The wind was light and the water plenty, and the mongoose them had sun in the afternoon.

"But one day some big machine come from town and gouge out the earth and pour a kind of sauce into the

wound. The sauce turn to stone and it soon had a big road—
not like these what you see here," she said, pointing down
at the shantytown streets, "but wide like ten of them together. A big big road what ain go no place."

Viggo squinted at this. "How you mean it ain go no
place?"

"It begin and it end," she tried to explain, "but it didn't
go nowhere. The machines them finish, and the great road
waited, but no car ain come."

"No car?"

"Not a one. But one afternoon your Great Uncle Eno
was sunning heself on a rock when out the sky he hear a
big commotion, a big-time roogoodoo." Here she stopped,
eyes wide, staring into the sky. "When he look up, he see
a strange machine fall out the sky and roll up on the great
road."

She spread her arms wide to look like this machine.
Clovis shifted his weight and drew closer. The night listened
in.

"Soon these thing falling out the sky everyday," she told
them. "Then the lagoon turned bad and the termite leave
their nest and the bird them fly away. The mongoose stay
there all the time hoping it go get better. Is only when they
see the bush shrinking back they decide to turn off. The
strong went north into the bush, and the smart went west
along the coast."

"What about Eno?" Viggo asked, already knowing but
not wanting the story to end.

"Now Eno wasn't smart and he wasn't strong," his mother
replied. "Eno went east. He tell me he hear rooster crowing
about a place where it have easy food. But when we reach

here, we find out we ain the first hear the news. From time Eno see more dog and cat and man and road up and down the place, he get scared. He carry me up this hill, talking all the time about how we go soon go back."

Here she closed her eyes, and Clovis gave Viggo a silent, knowing look.

"But Eno was too old to go home," she said, "and he ain had no home to go to anyway. To tell the truth, I think he even had like it up here."

"For true?" Viggo asked with a disapproving look around the churchyard.

"For true. But mind, Eno was no fool," she offered as a last thought. "In his youth your Great Uncle Eno was a sturdy fellow who live wild in the bush. And I ain talking bushes, child, I talking bush. Eno was one of the last wild ones. You could be proud of that."

Then she gave his ear a tender lick, her way of saying good night. Clovis gave him a wink, and Viggo uncurled, stretched, and went to his place in the roots.

His mother always ended Eno's story there, but Viggo knew the rest, even parts she hadn't told him. From Clovis he knew Eno had died and been carried off by a hawk. Months later a new mongoose came into the yard, "a lizard-eating rascal" he'd overheard her tell Clovis. That rascal, he later discovered, was his father. His mother never spoke to him about his father, so the only picture Viggo had of him was with a squiggly lizard disappearing into his face.

His father remained in the yard only a few days. Not long after his departure Viggo entered the world, wet and wormy, born in a hollow of the churchyard wall.

"You Done Ready Already"

Early the next morning two trucks rumbled into the churchyard filled with women, zinc tubs, and food. Decorations were hung, tables set, and fires made. Viggo and his mother observed the strange gathering from a distance. Later more trucks came with children and music. By noon the churchyard was crammed with people, noise, and odors too numerous and delicious to describe.

Viggo and his mother withdrew to the cactus patch to wait it out. All day chicken bones and ribs filled garbage cans and flew in the yard. After a month of scraps Viggo saw it as a kind of blessing. His mother was suspicious; she saw it as a sign. For the goats, who didn't care for the meat, the pestering children, or later a hoard of scavenging dogs, the day was agony.

After the last singing truckload had rumbled down the hill, Viggo and his mother returned cautiously to the yard. They gathered whatever flesh and bones the mongrels had missed and stored it in a hole in the wall. Then they tried to settle into the night. But the goats were in a state, chewing and nodding, tugging at the ends of their ropes. Clovis, weary and brooding, retired to the western gate.

Clovis was still there in the morning, and Viggo went with his mother to be with him. No one had much to say, so the three faced a fresh wind and watched it move goosebumps across the bay.

Viggo's mother went down the steps before the first

shops opened, and Clovis remained, looking east, with Viggo beside him. Viggo was used to the goat's silences and most mornings would excuse himself to settle into the long shadows of the hibiscus hedge. But today the silence weighed heavier than usual. Viggo tried to think of something to say, but Clovis was stirred to speak first. He spoke of being young and a goat, a long time ago in the mountain bush east of town.

"My mother was from east end," he said. "We climb cliff and run wild in the cactus and scrub. One day we get catch. First the man put we inside a fence. Later he separate us. I come across that ridge in a truck couple years ago."

Viggo looked at these hills the sun had just climbed from and tried to imagine what was on the other side. How far was far? he wondered. And his mother had come from a long way in the other direction. How far was that? Next to it his own churchyard world seemed trifling, and standing beside Clovis, Viggo caught for the first time a measure of his own smallness.

But Clovis's talk of the mountain emboldened him.

"Some day we going up mountain," he announced. "All the way in the bush."

"I know so," Clovis replied.

"You do?" Viggo asked, a bit surprised.

"Sure."

"But not till when I get brave," Viggo cautioned, watching the goat out of the corner of his eye. "Then I go be ready."

"You done ready already," Clovis informed him.

"To fight dog and cat?" Viggo protested.

"Ain got no dog and cat in the bush."

"For true?"

"Not in the bush. Is the bush you say you going, ain't it?"

"Uh-huh," Viggo murmured.

"And even if you meet a dog, don't mean you must fight him. I never see a dog could catch a mongoose yet."

Viggo was still trying to picture this dogless place. Truly, the bush was a hard place to imagine.

"Clovis?"

"What?"

"Goat does live in the bush, ain't it?"

"Wild ones live there, yes."

"All like in the mountain?"

"Some. But not all mountain is bush, you know. These hill up from town have road and garbage and thing. Pure bush hard to find."

Viggo looked at the mountains. It was all bush to him. It worried him to know Clovis felt he was already ready to go there. He hoped his mother didn't feel the same way.

"It look far, eh?" Viggo muttered.

"The mountain closer than you think," Clovis replied. "Long as you really want to get there. Come, I show you something."

Clovis led him to the roots of a nearby tamarind tree. There, making its way by inches, far from the sea, was a hermit crab in the shell of a whelk. Viggo had seen these tireless travelers before, and it amazed him that a shell that had once lived beneath the waves now wandered freely on top of the hill. He watched the shell take its obstacles—a root, a rock, a leaf—one by one.

"Don't slow him up," Clovis instructed when Viggo's nose went low for a closer look. "He have a certain somewhere he trying to get to."

That evening Viggo waited by the gate for his mother to return from the streets. Already she was late. The sun showed orange on the hills to the west, and the murmur of town was subsiding, only the far cry of the rooster rising over it. Above him the sky had deepened to twilight. He decided to tell a story, and, wrapping his tail in front of him, he pulled and picked at it, looking for a place to begin. But the stories were tired of themselves.

A long, low horn sounded across the harbor. Viggo looked toward it and saw a lone gull wheel and cry and dive into the dark water. A cool wind washed across his fur, and he imagined what it would be like to be a creature living beneath the waves of the sea. He pretended the first stars were the surface of the water breaking far above him. Turning, he saw Clovis approaching, striding silently across the yard.

"It have room up there for a old goat?" he asked, leaping effortlessly onto the wall beside Viggo. "Ah," he breathed. "See how clear the air is tonight."

"Uh-huh," Viggo said without thinking. Then, looking and seeing the land travel as far west as the horizon, he said, "Yes, it really clear for true."

"You could tell without self looking," Clovis said, closing his eyes, "by hearing how the rooster calls carry."

Viggo listened. "They sure make plenty noise," he said after a moment.

"You understand them?" Clovis asked.

"Not so much," Viggo admitted.

"That's why it sound like noise. Is fowl gossip," the goat explained. "They crowing about all what happen today. Listen close."

Viggo tried, but one call fell too fast on the one before.

Clovis began to translate. "A woman dog get turn out the yard . . . a graveyard cat had kitten . . . a donkey get cut up by a machete . . . swine sell in the market . . . a dog bite up a man leg. . . ."

All this had happened beyond his churchyard world. As Clovis spoke, Viggo took a sidelong glance at the old ram, at the knotted muscles of his shoulder and the wind trailing in the white wisps of his beard. As the sun blinked out on the horizon, Clovis grew silent, and together they listened to the last staccato reports from the coops. It was late, Viggo knew, and something was very, very wrong.

"I wonder where my mother is?" Viggo asked, staring down at the streets.

"She late," Clovis said, looking west.

They waited a while longer, peering into the deepening night, each with his own thoughts, each thinking the same thing.

"I know where she leave a bone from yesterday," Clovis said, breaking the silence.

"I think I go wait here a little longer," Viggo answered.

"I go bring it."

Clovis returned with the bone and then left the yard to go look for her. Viggo watched the ram descend the stone stairway until the darkness swallowed him and Viggo was left with the sound of his own heart thumping inside him.

The night was still and the silence wide, and many of the lights and shantytown flames had already died.

He went to work on his bone, his breathing in snorts, his mind for a moment lost in the marrow. But when the bone was gone and there was nothing left to chew, his worries crept back. He wished for someone to share them with, but the goats were sleeping and not a bird or lizard lingered in the tree. The street was empty, and even the garbage bin was deserted except for the long streetlight shadow of a sleeping cat. Only the stars were awake above the line of mountains, so Viggo turned to them. He imagined they knew where his mother was and would lead Clovis to her. He thought about the things they would talk about when she returned and of the laughing story she'd tell. And thinking of these things, he drifted off.

Later, as Viggo slept, the moon came up and showed its face in the bay. Later still the mountains glowed with it, and the church cast a shadow across the yard. Only when the moon's path was complete and the latest hours had turned to early ones—only then, and with only the stars as his witness, did Clovis return to the hill, weary and alone.

"The Bush Go Find You"

Viggo stayed on the wall all night and remained by the stairs the following morning, but his mother did not return. As the day wore on, his worry gave way to anger and to feeling sorry for himself. How could she leave him all alone? he wanted to know. What was he going to eat now and who would tell him stories? He could find no answers to these questions and the day seemed indifferent to his woes. It vexed him to hear the birds singing and to see lizards going about their business undisturbed. It even seemed unfair that the grass should continue to bend in the wind.

Viggo slept by Clovis that night, and during his sleep the anger lifted and a great sadness swept down. The instant his eyes opened he knew for certain and forever his mother was gone. He spent the day in a corner, warding away the grief by pretending she was still alive. He imagined himself coming to her rescue, challenging all who dared cross his path. Cats were wrestled into gutters and dogs given savage bites. Each time, in his imaginings, he found her alive near the garbage bin; and each time, over and over, he carried her tenderly home.

The morning of the third day Viggo gnawed genip seeds desperately, growing more restless and impatient. The birds' songs no longer angered him, but he envied their wings. Nothing remained for him in the churchyard. Clovis, without saying it, had helped Viggo understand this. He saw in the goats with the ropes around their necks something of his own situation. To spite all that was familiar and dear to him, he ate a worm and, hating it, ate another.

He had begun to appreciate his position. There was food only in the streets or beyond in the mountains; and the longer he debated his course, the weaker and less able he would become. He was pleased with himself for seeing things so clearly even though it alarmed him to see what he saw. The looming mountains that only days before seemed distant and dreamlike, a storyland world of bush and bravery, now beckoned him from a forgotten place inside.

That evening on the wall, with Clovis by his side, he spoke of them.

"If a animal—any animal—wanted to go up mountain, I wonder what way most safe to go?"

"North," Clovis responded without acknowledging the creature in question. "West might be look more safe, but north go get him in the bush faster."

"How you know when you reach?" Viggo asked.

"Reach where?"

"In the bush."

"That hard to say," Clovis replied. He rubbed his chin on his shoulder and chewed his lip. "The bush ain just a place," he explained. "Is something does get inside you. You could look for the bush and think you see it coming, but when it take you in, you forget you was looking to go there. You see?"

"Uh-huh."

"When you really in the bush, you don't really know it."

This made things no clearer to Viggo. If anything, the bush was now darker and more impenetrable than ever.

"Clovis?"

"Yes, Viggo."

"What if I reach up mountain all the way in the bush and I don't like it?"

"Then come back." Clovis smiled. "But you ain go know

if you don't self go. And don't forget, plenty mongoose living up mountain what ain living in the bush."

"How?"

"Some eating garbage. You can't live bush and eat garbage same time," Clovis explained. "Garbage like rope—it longer but it still got you by the neck. Stay away from garbage and stay away from town."

"Town bad?"

"Badder than bad. I pass above it once in a truck. The earth seal over, man and dog swarming like termite all over the place. Long as you keep north, you ain go run into town."

Then, without any prompting from Viggo, Clovis went on to describe the quickest and safest route to the mountains, the dangers he might encounter and the best ways to avoid them. It startled Viggo to hear Clovis talk so matter-of-factly about things that recently were unthinkable to him. And the old ram spoke in such a way that Viggo suddenly fancied he meant for him to go then, at that moment, without further hesitation. He felt his heart, small inside him, pressed flush against everything unknown. But his voice rose above his fear.

"I don't think I ready to go today," he said.

"No call to rush," Clovis assured him. "Leave when you ready to leave, and don't be in no hurry to get where you think you wanting to go. Enjoy the road as you go along. That is the best."

The day Viggo left to go to the mountains, dawn broke to a cloudless sky and gentle winds. He spent the morning with Clovis, reviewing details of the journey. The goats, aware that Viggo was leaving, were on their feet and more alert than usual. They were excited for him and wished him well.

In the afternoon Viggo ate some papaya, sucked milk from a she-goat, and fell asleep at Clovis's side. When he awoke, he went to look for a last time at the corner he and his mother had called home. Then Clovis led him through the cactus patch to a windswept promontory overlooking the bay. Viggo was to go down the south side of the hill, east along the shoreline, then north through the streets just after dusk.

The view from the rocks was new to him. The sea was wider than he'd seen it before, blue beyond thought. Clovis said nothing, allowing the scene to cast its spell.

"You think someday you might go back to the bush too?" Viggo asked.

Clovis looked out at the bay.

"I got to think about the other goat them," he answered. "I done spend a good bit of time in the bush already. And, in a way, I still there."

"In the bush?"

"Once you been there, the bush goes where you go," Clovis said. "Long as I eating grass and ain got no rope around my neck, I go be all right. Up mountain is best, but I ain the young ram I once was."

Clovis paused to consider the wind. Viggo looked out too, but not seeing what the old goat saw, his eyes fell to the stone Clovis stood on. His hooves were fused to the stone, the stone wedged in the earth, and the earth laced with roots. Viggo was in the roots himself.

"Clovis?" he asked.

"Yes, Viggo."

"My father was a lizard-eater?"

The question made the goat laugh. "I suppose he ate them," he said. "Most mongoose do."

"They do?" Viggo exclaimed.

"Sure. Maybe your mother ain like them, but most mongoose swallow them right down."

"You had know him good?" Viggo asked.

"Not so good because he ain stay here long. But I had like him. He had think like a goat."

"For true?"

"For true. Your mother too. If they was here, they maybe might tell you the same thing I done tell you already."

"What thing?"

"Not to be running up and down the place looking for the bush. Enjoy the road, and the bush go find you."

Below them a pelican flapped against the wind, rising slowly to their height, and held motionless in the buffeting breeze. Viggo and Clovis watched this aerial display, and the pelican seemed to know it. Then a gust got under his wing and tilted him, and he swooped west and out of sight.

A silent tremor deep in his chest told Viggo the time had come. He looked up at Clovis, and his eyeball got a goat lick intended for his head. They both laughed.

"Sorry," Clovis said. Then he landed a good rough wet one on Viggo's head—just like his mother used to do.

"Now," Clovis said, growing serious. He swelled his chest and held his horns high. "Show me how you look."

Viggo puffed himself up, narrowed his eyes, and showed

his teeth, looking just as fierce as he could. Clovis studied him from head to toe.

"Yeah, Viggo, you looking good."

"Thank you, Clovis," Viggo said, himself again.

"Now go quick," Clovis ordered, "and get yourself from this place."

Where Most People End

Viggo worked down the slope, his mind curiously empty, his feet feeling their way. He moved along the trail, allowing his eyes to focus on nothing new or unfamiliar. In minutes the covering of scrub ended, and the trail broke into the blinding shorelight. He lingered for a moment in the shade with the shadowy forms that inhabited it. One sinewy mangrove tree stood at the mouth of the path like a sentinel at the gate. The trunk offered only silence, but a bough lifted in the wind as if to open the way.

He wound east through the shore boulders until he came to the road Clovis told him about. He crouched in the weeds studying it. It was as if a great stone belt was cinched into the earth so tightly that nothing could grow. He examined its length, fearing it, and began to suspect it was alive—like a gigantic snake. When a truck passed, the road moved beneath the wheels, and dust, like a serpent's breath, rose and fell through the air. Viggo decided he was not yet ready to cross it.

He curled up between a water catchment and a large cistern waiting for the sun to go down. Toward dusk a slight drizzle produced a trickle in the cistern, and the water's sound stirred his memory. He drifted back to his mother's stories of bush and beasts and brave ancestors. Last among them was his Great Uncle Eno as Viggo imagined him, young and sturdy and strong.

When he surfaced from this reverie, he arose and, with renewed spirit, marched to the road.

"I ain fraid of no road," he declared, edging up to it. The serpent appeared to be sleeping. With a mighty mongoose dash he shot across it and headed north.

He moved along a winding path past sheds and shanties and overturned boats, keeping his head low. He entered a culvert that skirted a field and stayed in the high grass that grew there until he emerged beside a yard of abandoned cars—a fearful place where twisted frames lay in heaps. On the other side was the main waterfront road. He summoned his courage and bolted across it, through a flood of light, and into some tall guinea grass on the far side.

The road was so hard and the light so bright that Viggo fancied the worst was already behind him and that the grass was the beginning of the mountains. But a sudden wall stopped him short.

He went east and then west, trying to find a way around it, but the wall went on and on without end. He found a bush growing beside it, scrambled up and leaped from a low limb to the top of the wall. In the depths beneath the trees—trees taller than any he'd seen before—his eyes beheld a strange place hemmed in on all sides and crowded with

shapes and forms he had no name for. Tombs and crosses, statues and vaults loomed as far as he could see. Huge tamarind and mahogany trees mushroomed out of the earth, their roots corkscrewing into the dark soil. Winged men in robes of white stone stood guard.

"Clovis ain tell me nothing about this," he said beneath his breath. He leaped from the wall to a high tomb protected by a large statue and stared down the silent rows.

"Don't leave me catch no tomcat around here tonight," he called out at the darkness.

A cool wind answered him, giving the tamarind pods a dry rattle. Then he felt the first pellets of rain. He curled up beneath the broad stone hem of the statue and tucked his tail in. It would not be so bad a place to spend the night he decided, looking around. He was starting his adventures where most people end theirs, but he was high and dry, and the graveyard figures were somehow comforting.

A sudden jolt of lightning crashed in on his thoughts. He looked up through the statue's outstretched arms. To the east the stars were going black, and he could hear the sound of a downpour moving in. Looking for better shelter, he leaped to the wall and followed it until it led to a street-light. Then the rain began in earnest.

The street was empty. He jumped down and ran into a covered gutter, pleased to have found a place so dry. But the rain continued in torrents, and the water that flowed in the gutter began to rise. He continued into the twisting darkness beneath the street, losing his sense of direction. Twigs and cans shot past him, and just when he was running out of ceiling room and feared he would drown, the gutter opened into a wide basin where other rivers of rainwater converged. He climbed onto a narrow ledge beneath an overhang and waited.

What would become of him now? he wondered.

Suddenly the thrashing body of a huge rat sped past him, drawn into the whirlpool. The rodent turned circles in the basin, fighting for a foothold. In the second before he disappeared, the rat caught Viggo's eye in a final fruitless plea for help. Then he was gone.

Viggo forgot his fear of rain. He climbed out of the gutter and stood shocked and bewildered to see where the storm gutters had carried him. He was on a corner, with corridors of tall buildings branching out in several directions. He looked up each street. At the end of one was the promising sight of a tree, and he ran blindly toward it, hoping the street would deliver him. He raced through a jumble of sidewalks and signs, where the windows stared down on him and the walls echoed the storm.

When the street finally ended, Viggo found himself in a wide tree-filled square with buildings on all sides. A maze of streets emptied into the square, each more threatening than the other. He decided to go no deeper into the town. Between two buildings he found a tight crawlspace that was dry. He worked his way beneath a canvas tarp and up into a bag that was snug and warm. Outside, the storm raged on.

Viggo remained wide-eyed in the dark bottom of the bag for what seemed a very long time. When the rain stopped, he looked out on the square from the mouth of the alley and considered running in the direction he'd come from.

But three dogs crossing on the far side helped change his mind.

Instead, he took a moment to investigate the alley. It was narrow, not much wider than a good-size dog. He studied a hibiscus bush, a leaky downspout, and a pan collecting water. Then he inspected the alley's bottles and cans. At the far end he heard rummaging sounds and smelled a strong, unpleasant odor. Though that end was sealed shut by a wall, a thin column of light showed where there was a missing brick.

He put his eye to the opening. There, only a few yards away, twin bins of garbage overflowed into a moat of trash. A pack of dogs nosed through it while cats made forays from the roofs. Most of the dogs were bigger than the ones he'd seen in the churchyard, but it was a short bulldog— blind on one side and a blue eye on the other—who called the shots. This one toyed with a huge bone and kept the blue eye on all who came and went. Viggo saw a doe-eyed mongrel come into the light—a mother, judging from the slack breasts. The blue eye fell across her, and she slowed her approach, then struck a pose—her ribs showing—and pretended to scratch. The blue-eyed beast went back to his bone, allowing the mother to cower closer toward a promising scrap. He let her sniff just once, then bared his teeth and lunged at her.

Viggo was back trembling beneath the tarp before her cries had faded up the street. Only hours before he'd stood beside Clovis overlooking the bay. He wanted to know what nature of place he'd come to and why. He retraced his steps from Clovis to the seashore and from the cemetery to the storm, looking for the missed turn. He wanted to know which way was out and how deep into the place he'd fallen.

He'd fallen deeply indeed. He'd landed in the market-place, in the very soul of town.

Ziggy and Johnny Cakes

Sounds slanted into Viggo's sleep like a cast of strange acquaintances. When he awoke, it was to the sound of a truck. He heard it rumble toward him from some distance, then felt its headlights sweep across his alley and, for an instant, burst into his bag. The truck came to a stop outside, and the engine went off. A long moment of silence followed. Viggo braced himself and, in his mongoose way, prepared for the worst.

Two doors slammed. There were voices and the sounds of things being unloaded. A moment later the truck started up. Viggo listened with relief as it backed off and pulled away. But someone was still outside. He could hear movements and shuffling about. Then a woman's voice began to sing. He was about to peek out when the song came closer and the tarp was suddenly dragged away. A delicious scent found its way into the bag.

Viggo shifted and the bag moved. The singing stopped. He waited in the silence until the melody resumed. Then, by inches, he stole to the mouth of the bag, his eyes searching out the sweet-smelling thing. Instead, his eyes met the eyes of a woman sorting her wares, still in her tune but with her eye on the bag.

Viggo ducked back and waited. He had never been so close to a person and was mad at having shown his face. Then her soft music came toward him again, and he heard her arms in the limbs of the hibiscus bush above him.

"Let me pick some of these flowers, pretty up the place," she said. He smelled the good thing on her. Then a piece of it—a good-size piece—dropped from her hand right into his bag. It came to rest on his rear paw.

Still, he watched her. She was brown and round like her sacks, and the things she pulled from them were the color and shape of her song. He watched her hook the tarp to the wall and draw it across her fruits and vegetables. She made a last quick hitch, and her song stopped.

"Look like you never taste a johnnycake before," she said, looking at him. Her voice had shifted out of the song. He studied her, not understanding the sounds she made.

"Eat the thing," she insisted. She took one herself and bit into it.

Her song started again and Viggo kept a vigilant eye on her every movement. Twice she looked over her shoulder to see how he was getting along. When she looked a third time, Viggo's teeth were into the brown crust. It was doughy inside and still warm, he discovered—just as a good johnnycake should be.

When he'd finished it and licked his paws and whiskers clean, she put a small wooden bowl of something next to the downspout inside his alley. He bristled his hair and made a brave show of his teeth, but when she had turned her back, he lapped up what the bowl had to offer. He had already decided to postpone his escape to the mountains because the market was now too busy and too dangerous. Besides, he wasn't yet sure which direction the mountains were. All that was clear to him was that he was between two buildings in a long well of stone with, above it, only a sliver of sky crossed by wires and vines.

But the alley seemed safe. There was food and a good view of wheels and feet and things he'd never imagined. He saw a bicycle, a cement mixer, and a long line of children dressed in green and white. He marveled at how easily people moved about on only two legs and with hair sprouting straight out of the tops of their heads. Their sounds were quite peculiar—nothing like a dog or a goat or a bird—and one person was not even like another. He heard high voices and low, laughter and song, and understood none of it.

Viggo saw a boy approaching the stall. He wore shorts, a T-shirt cut off above the belly, an orange cap turned sideways, and no shoes. He carried a stack of paper.

"Morning, Ziggy," he greeted the marketwoman.

Ziggy looked up. "Selwin, you early today."

The boy handed her a newspaper and Ziggy fished some coins out of her apron and gave them to him along with a johnnycake.

"News stale," he said, taking a bite.

"Look so," she said, glancing at it and putting it to one side. "Oh! I near forget. Look."

She pointed at the alley. The newsboy followed her finger and met Viggo's eye.

"A mongoose?"

"I meet him there this morning," she smiled. "From time I give him piece of johnnycake look like he ain going no place."

"Mongoose in the market?" the boy exclaimed. "No one ain go harass him?"

She grasped a pan by the handle. "Anyone look to humbug him, I go hit them one of these!"

"See how he sitting up and thing!" the boy exclaimed. "I could give him piece of caramel?"

"See if he go eat it." Ziggy shrugged.

Viggo watched the boy reach into his pocket and unwrap something. Then he crouched and tossed it into his bowl. Viggo gave it a cursory sniff and gobbled it up. The little cube required serious chewing.

"That go keep him busy," Ziggy said.

"Tomorrow I go bring a chocolate."

"Bring it, yes."

For a moment they admired Viggo's efforts. He was still smacking and slurping, but he had most of it down.

"Okay, Ziggy. I going up."

"Tell your mother hello and tell her bring the bottles."

"I go tell her," the boy said, turning to go.

"Okay, then."

"All right."

The boy waved at Viggo, and Viggo watched him disappear into the crowd. Then another person stepped up and pointed at the papayas. Ziggy unfolded a bag and put two in, singing her song.

By the time the truck returned to gather away the woman and her food, Viggo was numb from all the saltfish and johnnycake and stew he'd eaten. He hid beneath the tarp until the truck was gone and then came out to find she'd left him a last helping of stew. He wolfed it down, not pausing to savor the mutton or the tanya or to marvel how the dumplings floated in the sauce. When only a hefty bone remained, he ventured onto the sidewalk to sniff and see if any stew had slopped out of the pot. As luck would have it, some had. He applied his tongue to the dribbles on the pavement and scarfed up a wayward carrot. He felt quite pleased with himself for being so clever.

He went back to the alley and curled up with the bone for a bit of reflective gnawing. The market square was cloaked in twilight, its silent stalls lidded with shadows. It was hard to believe this was the same place he'd arrived at terror-stricken in a storm the night before. Was this the same town Clovis had warned him about? he wondered. In one day he'd eaten so much he was surprised by the weight of his own belly. It was as if he'd not yet waked from a dream.

This was not to say he'd forgotten about the mountain and his journey to the bush.

"I ain forget about that," he assured himself, talking to the downspout on the corner of a building. But when he tried to sense the direction of the mountains, he could think only of the frightening corridors he'd have to go through to get there. It wouldn't hurt, he decided, polishing off the bone, to stay another day. Just long enough to fatten up for his trip to the bush.

A Blue-Eyed Visitor

After a night of cats leaping arcs on the roofs and roaches parading up the downspout, the truck finally returned. He saw Ziggy unload it, with a tall bony man with a pinched, unsmiling face. When the truck was gone, she went beneath some folds and produced a ladle of something for him. He was less cautious than the day before and wasted no time getting his face into the bowl.

"You looking well bold today," she observed. "That's saltfish you eating. Tomorrow is bullfoot, Friday is kallaloo, and Saturday is souse," she informed him, counting on her fingers.

While she set up, Viggo looked out at the market and saw people and things he'd seen the day before. The same woman was setting out her vegetables across from them, and when she was done, the same gray cat curled up around her feet. The newsboy who gave him the caramel returned, this time with a sweet brown ball of chocolate. When the sugarcane cart passed, Viggo's head turned small circles trying to follow the wheel, and he realized with a grin that his head had turned the same circles the day before. The familiar sights made him feel safe, and the hot dumpling in his mouth gave him a warm feeling inside.

Later, when the sun was overhead and had found its way even to the bottom of his alley, a line of people formed at Ziggy's stall. Viggo watched her ladle out portions, content to know he'd already eaten two helpings of the very thing people were waiting in line for. Some of them seemed to recognize him from the day before, and one kind customer even placed a bit of meat in his bowl. Surely Clovis had misjudged these creatures.

At one point the marketwoman held out a bone and Viggo stood on his hind legs for it. This little trick produced squeals of delight from her and her customers. In fact, Viggo quickly noticed that the more who came to the stall to watch, the more tidbits he seemed to get. He ended up spending much of the lunch hour on his hind legs. He wondered how people could walk this way all day and why it never occurred to them to use all four.

Before she left that afternoon, Ziggy gave Viggo his first coconut tart, easily the best thing he'd ever tasted. Out of it grew a vision, a sudden inspiration. Could it be, he wondered, that the market was the very place, the promised land of easy food his Great Uncle Eno had heard about from roosters? Had he, Viggo, stumbled upon it and had Eno just not traveled far enough? This was food for thought.

And there was something else, something he'd been hiding from, that the coconut tart now forced him to consider. Suppose he finally did make his escape to the mountain only to discover the bush was a hardscrabble place, a luckless life of lizard eating and toil? Of course, his mother's bush stories made it seem like the only place a mongoose could find contentment. But what mongoose would prefer lizards to warm stew? he asked himself. And what mongoose would not wish to have his bowl? The coconut tart was making him see these matters very clearly.

After he finished it, he fell asleep. He dreamed he was in the bush, a green dream of leaves and earth. In a forest

clearing high on the mountain he saw other mongooses, each with his own wooden bowl. In this dream forest the boughs dripped with tarts and candy.

When he awoke, he felt out of sorts. Perhaps it was the narrowness of the alley, he told himself, or the wad of goo in his belly. He tried to sleep, but there was a loud rumpus in the garbage bin nearby. He was also troubled by certain thoughts, bothersome wonderings about the bush that he could blunt only by chewing a large, uneatable bone. Then, when he could chew no more and was just drifting off, he heard something.

Sniffing the pavement outside was the bulldog, the blue-eyed bully he'd seen his first night in town. He nosed right up to the alley and tried to get at Viggo's bowl, but his head was too thick to get past the downspout. He sniffed again and peered in, then showed his blind eye, lifted his leg, and parted with a snort.

Viggo watched him saunter through the streetlight. The dog turned into a silhouette, became a shadow, then disappeared.

Orville

Though Viggo still planned to strike out for the mountains, the pleasures of town seemed to have a way of delaying his departure. Each night he vowed anew to leave the following morning. Then he'd oversleep and, after his morning meal, decide instead to leave that night. In this way his time in town wore on.

Several days after his encounter with the bulldog, Viggo was cooling himself beneath Ziggy's awning and watching the market close. He felt a good deal more relaxed than he had his first day in town. He'd cleared his alley of bottles and cans, and Ziggy had set up a snappy cardboard box for him to sleep in. More than once he caught himself wishing Clovis and his other churchyard chums could see him now.

It was Saturday, the biggest market day, and Ziggy had arrived that morning with several shiny pots of conch and whelk. As if that wasn't excitement enough, Viggo had seen a wailing red fire truck, a man selling balloons, and his first donkey, a huge swayback creature several times the size of a goat. It was his most exciting day of all.

"Got to count the money," Ziggy said, elbow deep in burlap.

He watched her pull out a small, flat box and take the money and coins from her apron. This meant the truck would soon be there. She counted it aloud. Each evening this was the last thing she did, and her soft numbers landed on Viggo's ears like a lullaby.

"Twenty-one, twenty," it ended. "Twenty-one, twenty," she repeated, committing it to memory.

The rumble of the truck could be heard in the distance. She gave him a tweak and a scratch behind the ear and pulled the tarp over his box. Through a window of canvas he watched them load the truck and saw the man's eye pass over the alley in a final check. But Viggo was too deep in the shadows to be seen. The truck backed up, and he saw Ziggy give him a little wave as they drove away.

When it was gone, Viggo came out to watch the last people packing up. It had been a busy afternoon, and the air was heavy with spilled food and rotting fruit that had baked in the sidewalk sun all day. A gust of wind swept through, and eddies of plastic and paper swirled across the square. A lone can rolled down the street with a mind of its own and came to rest in the gutter. Across the market Viggo spotted the donkey he'd seen that morning, and he jumped to the window ledge for a better look.

The creature was heaped with bundles, a chair clumsily lashed to his back. A man tightened a rope around the donkey's neck and pulled, but the beast refused to move. Then he took the end of the rope and began whipping the donkey. The animal lurched to one side and several things fell off and clattered to the pavement. The man struck the donkey again and again. Why didn't he fight back? Viggo wondered. If he was the donkey, he would certainly give the man a good kick!

After the man and the donkey were gone, Viggo got his frenzied teeth into a piece of cardboard and thrashed about in his box, wishing he could bite the man's nose off. Only when he bit his own tongue by mistake did he realize the state he'd gotten himself into. He peeked out of his box. He was relieved to see no one had observed his strange behavior.

When the marketwoman failed to show up the next morning, Viggo began to understand the extra food she'd left in his bowl. This was part of the meaning of Sunday. The other part had to do with garbage, which, uncollected for two days, overflowed the bins and gave rise to fights. At dawn, hymns rose inside the church across the square. But outside the vermin ruled, and every roach and rat and dog and cat muscled in for a cut of the trash.

It was no longer a secret that his alley was occupied and that he was the creature living beneath the tarp. The pavement around his bowl was so soaked in stew juices that not even a dumb dog thinking of a distant garbage can could fail to pick up the scent. With all of the canine activity, Viggo decided this would be a good day to stay put.

First he amused himself by sorting through a collection of candy the newsboy had given him, hoping their colors and lively wrappings would brighten his day. He soon grew tired of this. He longed to talk with another creature. Without the marketwoman's songs he realized how silent his alley world was. To fill the silence he fell into reciting his mother's stories. He was surprised how fresh and vivid these tales were after so long a time. The scenes he painted filled his darkness and once again renewed in him a yearning for the bush. He was full of the most noble mongoose intentions.

Suddenly, there was sniffling outside. Fearing the bulldog, he peered out under the canvas flap and saw a short scruffy dog instead. The dog squeezed past the downspout and, with a deft twist of his tongue, maneuvered a pork bone into his mouth.

"That's my bone you eating," Viggo announced, poking his nose through the flap.

"Sorry," the dog said, backing away. Then, when he saw Viggo more clearly, he trotted off.

"Hey!" Viggo called after him.

The dog stopped and looked back.

"Is all right," Viggo said, eager now to be friendly.

"You finish?" the fuzzy face asked.

"From last night," Viggo assured him, his own voice new to him, like a stranger in his throat. He nudged the bowl past the downspout and the dog got his nose into it. He had distinguished whiskers on one end and a balding red rump on the other. He gulped it all down, saving the tanya for last.

"Good," he said, licking his whiskers. "Is a long time you living in there?"

"Not so long."

"First I ever see a mongoose living in a alley," the dog mused.

"You know about mongoose?" Viggo asked.

"I use to live up mountain," the dog answered. "Plenty mongoose up there."

"You use to live up mountain?"

"Until last year," the dog answered. "Where you from?"

Viggo wasn't quite sure where he was from.

"From the west," he answered in a small voice. The dog squinted at this.

"My name is Orville," he said. "What yours own is?"

"Viggo," Viggo answered with certainty.

"That's a nice name." The dog smiled. "You want us go by the waterfront, Viggo?"

"Where that is?"

"Down so," Orville answered, tilting his head south.

"For what?" Viggo asked, reluctant to venture from the alley.

"Fish guts!" Orville barked with a mad wag.

"Fish guts?" Viggo frowned. He looked Orville over closely to be sure he hadn't missed something.

"You is a friend of the blue-eye dog?" he asked.

"Hannibal?"

"The fat head one," Viggo explained.

"Hannibal," the dog repeated.

"You is his friend?"

Orville raised a bushy eyebrow and stepped back.

"I look like Hannibal friend to you?"

"I fraid dog," Viggo said.

"Don't be fraid," Orville replied. "I does like mongoose."

They crossed the market and headed down an alley similar to Viggo's, though bigger. The overhead gutters and vines and shuttered windows were all familiar to him, and so were the weeds sprouting from the walls. Even Orville felt like an old friend walking beside him. But when the alley ended and the echoes fell away, Viggo entered a great sphere of blue where the harbor fused blue with the sky. As he walked toward the water, he felt the mountains rising behind him; and when Orville stopped to sniff, Viggo turned to face them.

They were nearer than he'd ever seen them. Green slopes rose out of the roofs of town, shouldering each other east and west as far as he could see. Every valley and twisting ridge was distinct, but it was difficult for him to look at. To see it so close and to know he'd failed to get there made it seem doubly distant and unreachable. The mountains looked down on him and seemed to say, "So, we see each other."

Viggo turned and looked seaward. A banana boat lay listless at its mooring, flag without wind, sail drooping from the boom. Though above him a lid seemed to have been lifted, the blue of the sky carried its own weight and pressed down on him a feeling of wasted time.

Orville returned, his face smelling of fish. He showed Viggo the part of the mountains where he was from and told how he'd been abandoned there as a puppy. He knew the hills above town and was a veteran of many trash bin skirmishes. He'd lived in town only a year. All this he related in a moment with a shrug and a wag.

Viggo's story did not unfold as quickly. So starved was he to talk, he told Orville everything. He explained how he'd struck out for the mountain to live wild in the bush like a real mongoose. He told him about the storm and the place with the stone statues and about his good fortune to land in the market. Then he offered descriptions of every dish he'd eaten, caught up with the sound of his own voice.

"So when you going up?" Orville cut in.

"Up?"

"You ain say you going mountain?"

"Oh," Viggo answered, "that." He was annoyed to have his description of mutton stew interrupted.

"I soon going," he said, feeling the mountains' silence.

"Soon when?" Orville asked.

"You want me tell about mutton stew or what?" Viggo asked, up on his hind legs.

"If you want to talk about it, go ahead," Orville sighed. "But I taste goat plenty time already."

"But is mutton I talking about."

"So what you think mutton is?" Orville asked with a smile.

"Goat?"

"Goat."

This news brought Viggo off his hind legs. He stared at the banana boat turning on its mooring, its flag fluttering a bit. He was thinking of Clovis. He did not want to talk about food anymore.

"I soon going up, yes."

"Good," Orville replied. "Just don't leave anything happen to you all the while."

"Anything like what?"

"You forget about Hannibal?"

"The bulldog?"

"Yes. And that ain all. You see this?" Orville showed him the raw spot on his rump, a crease still deep in the flesh. "I was just walking up the road and then—*bragadam!*—a big rockstone lick me down."

"How it hit you?" Viggo asked.

"How?" Orville exclaimed. "A fellow throw it, no! Your belly too full of stew. Don't mind some woman feeding you all the time. Not all so good. Man easy to like but hard hard to trust."

Viggo was staring at the water, thinking about the man he'd seen beating the donkey.

"And a next thing."

"What?"

"Don't be walking around on your hind leg," Orville advised. "Stay low or in the gutter."

"You want me hide all the time?" Viggo asked.

"No," Orville shook his head. "Stand up for your rights. But if you ain ready to fight, best be ready to run."

Viggo was staring at Orville as if he'd forgotten who Orville was, a blank look on his face.

"You want us go up by where I live?" Orville asked, changing the subject.

"Huh?"

"I say you want us go up by where I live?"

"Where?"

"By the gut."

"What that is?" Viggo asked, still somewhere else.

"Where the rain run off the mountain," Orville answered, trying to hold Viggo's eye.

"It far from here?"

"East from the market."

"It safe?"

Hearing this question seemed to please Orville.

"Safer than the market. You could be sure of that."

Walking from the water, Viggo again faced the mountains. They stirred the same mongoose longings. But when he and Orville entered the alleyway the mountains disappeared, the buildings reclaimed him, and the longings went away.

The Gut

They walked east. The route narrowed and grew darker, and new odors crowded in on them. Laughter emptied from doorways, and old men stared from stoops; Viggo stayed close to Orville, his eyes straight ahead. At one corner, where the street widened, there was a well and a woman drawing water.

"Over here," Orville directed.

Viggo followed him between two boards, beneath a bush, and up an embankment. He heard the voice of rushing water. The other side dropped into a deep gully where water tumbled down a chute. On the far side another wall rose again to street level.

"This is the gut," Orville said over the roar.

Viggo saw a large tire being hustled down the rapids, chased by a broken board. Both bounced willy-nilly over the boulders and shot into the darkness beneath the bridge.

"Usually it dry," Orville said. "Must be raining up mountain. I does live up the gut round couple bend."

"Up the gut?" Viggo frowned, thinking about the rat he'd seen swept into the whirlpool.

"If you follow me you go be safe."

"I ain going in there," Viggo replied.

"No?"

"Not me,"

"Maybe a next time, then," Orville suggested. "When the water ain running so hard."

"Maybe a next time, yes."

"Good. It ain so bad," Orville assured him. "Watch as I go up and you go see."

Viggo nodded.

"You know how to reach back to the market, ain't it?"

Viggo nodded again.

"And don't forget what I tell you. Stay in the gutter and out of trouble," Orville advised.

"I won't forget."

"But stand up for your rights."

"I go stand up, yes," Viggo said with a worried look.

"See you, then."

"See you."

Orville sidestepped down a steep slope to the water's edge. Then, sticking close to the wall, he started up the gut. Viggo watched him vanish and reappear between boulders, skirting the raging water. Where the gut turned north, he stopped and gave Viggo a parting bark, then disappeared around the bend.

Back in his alley, Viggo found his bowl licked clean by cockroaches. He unwrapped a caramel and hunkered down in his box. It had been a long day, and there was a lot to think about. He put his jaws to work.

The places Orville had taken him reminded Viggo there was more to the world than his alleyway. No longer was there any question about the direction of the mountains. They were north, a few blocks from where he lay hiding in his cardboard box. So the question clouded in on him: with the mountain so close and the bush before him, what was keeping him in town?

He knew it was strange and unmongooselike, but the town had grown on him. He loved easy food, of course, but there was more to it than that. He enjoyed the marketplace and the way his days had a beginning and a middle and an end. He liked how one gutter led to another and the way cracks and sharp edges were neatly sealed over with mortar or stone. Though a part of him still longed for the mountain, it was not easy to put aside his cozy notion that he was a very lucky mongoose.

But the gut had changed that. The rushing water had found him out, touched him where he was most deeply a mongoose. He'd seen it tear through town, carving beneath roadbed and foundation, laying bare the red earth. It was as if the water was a voice bearing him a message from the mountain.

But what was it? What was it the water made him feel? Viggo asked himself this question over and over in the darkness beneath the tarp. His heart knew the answer was inside him. But it was a deep thing, quick and slippery, and not yet ready to be caught.

Standing Up for His Rights

When he awoke the next morning, the memory of the day before was still fresh. But he found the mountain hard to bring to mind. Though he'd seen it only the day before, his thoughts would travel no further than the brick and plaster in front of his nose. He quietly debated the matter with the wall, but the wall couldn't help him, so he stopped trying. Later he was heartened when the marketwoman arrived, singing a song, with a fresh batch of johnnycakes and a ladle of stew. Then the streetsweepers came, and the garbage truck came, and it was as if Sunday never was. He'd forgotten the simple pleasures of his bowl, a rolling wheel, and a calypso song. He was remembering the side of the market he liked.

But at lunch he was forced to remember the other side when he looked up from a hefty serving of kallaloo to see Hannibal sniffing the pavement behind Ziggy's feet. The bulldog's white eye shone like a half-moon beneath a fold of skin. When he saw Viggo, he turned to hide the dead eye and show only the blue, and he bent his mouth into a quick smile. The eye went from Viggo to his bowl and back.

"Hello," he said, giving Viggo his best profile.

"Good day," Viggo said, looking up from his food. The bulldog was clearly too fat to get into the alley. He remembered what Orville said about standing up for his rights.

"Nice little house you have there," the bulldog said in a husky voice. "And a good bowl of food to boot." The blue eye glinted with kindness.

"It tastes good too," Viggo said with a neighborly smile. He felt safe inside the narrow alley. He took another bite, making an excellent show of how good it was. Hannibal eyed him.

"I know where it have some good bone," the dog whispered with a gush of foul breath.

"I have a bone already," Viggo answered.

"These have on more meat," the bulldog assured him.

Viggo pretended not to hear this, but he could not play his part much longer. He cleaned his whiskers and tried to appear calm while his heart somersaulted in his chest.

"Come," Hannibal insisted in his most reasonable voice. "They right over here. Come, I show you."

"No," Viggo said firmly.

The bluntness of his reply took some of the twinkle out of the blue eye. Hannibal sat back on his haunches. His smile cracked and his lip slipped off his biggest tooth.

"Well, why don't you come out here anyway so I could get a better look at you," he said. "First I ever see a mongoose so close."

"And this is close as you go see me," Viggo said, his hair beginning to bristle. The blue eye narrowed.

"You like to make joke?" Hannibal asked.

"I ain making joke," Viggo answered.

"Well, when I get my teeth into you, you go see what kind of joke *I* making." He snarled, showing his great fangs, and lunged at the alley's opening. The downspout shook but held firm. Folds of skin gathered against it and a smear of foam ran down.

"Get your blasted backside from here!" Ziggy yelled, grazing Hannibal with a broom handle. He growled and glared at Viggo once more.

"Out!" Ziggy screamed again, this time connecting with a full swing. The bulldog yelped and trotted off, drawing heckles from other vendors and, from one man, a red piece of rotting fruit. But the missile missed wide and exploded on the market steps.

♦

It took all afternoon for Viggo's insides to settle. He was not sorry to have said what he had because the bulldog couldn't be put off by kind words. But now he knew his days in town were numbered and that he would have to follow Orville's advice to stick to gutters and alleys too narrow for his thick-headed tormentor. And if he was going to escape to the mountains, he would have to make his move soon.

When Ziggy was gone and the market was empty, he slipped away. He went north through the market and east into the backstreet gutter; three blocks beneath the sidewalk and left at the clogged drain; finally north again through the grating and east to the light by the well. He listened for a moment, then looked both ways and trotted past the well, through the split plank, under the bushes, and up the bank to the top of the wall.

It was just as Orville told him. Tonight there was only a dizzy trickle in the center of the gut. He looked both ways and, seeing no danger, sidestepped down the trail. As he descended into the gut, the lights of town faded until it seemed town had risen into the night sky and flown away, leaving him not in town at all but in some wild riverbed. He weaved through the boulders, getting his paws wet, and crossed a fallen tree trunk to the gut's far side. He went as far as the bend where Orville had disappeared the night before. There the walls narrowed and forked, and clothes-lines colored the sky.

He scrambled up the biggest boulder he could find and looked back down the gut. He was feeling very much like a real mongoose—or at least the way he imagined a real mongoose might feel. Over the line of rooftops he saw a thin sliver of moonlight in the bay. The roosters were having a last go of it, and they brought to mind his old friend Clovis. He wondered if perhaps the old ramgoat could hear the same rooster cries at that moment.

The memory of Clovis remained with him and gave rise to certain wonderings that kept him up half the night, lingering with the wet scent of root and earth and the soft singing sounds of water moving through stone.

Manteoba

Overnight the gut became a friend to Viggo and a passageway to other places. Often during the day he went there, leaving the market for no greater joy than to be out of the place. Ziggy noticed these departures and did nothing to discourage them, sensing perhaps that Viggo was happier going wherever it was he went. The incident with the bulldog had frightened her. The market was no place for a mongoose, and she knew her feeding him was what kept him there.

Viggo loved coming and going in the gut. He was a contented mongoose, happy with himself and pleased with his place in things. When it rained, he ran to see water run off the mountain. He gloried in the rough-and-tumble world of the gut, with its sticks and stones and bush enough to give him the feeling of the mountain without all the effort of the climb. He was at peace, becalmed by it all, perfectly willing to let the world of town whirl on without him.

He still worried about the bulldog, however, and he still made special efforts to avoid him. The efforts brought to mind his old churchyard fears of fighting, and to confront them he once again began practicing to be brave. His favorite place to do this was on a slope where a steep stone face overlooked the gut. Usually he sat atop a clump of moss and let his mind wander. He liked to pretend the trunks of trees were great bush adversaries afraid to do battle with him. Sometimes he imagined the gut to be a wild river, and from the edge of the cliff he'd strike a grand pose and open his arms to this imagined domain.

Late one afternoon when he was striking his great hunter's pose, he saw a dog staring up at him.

"Orville," Viggo said, a bit embarrassed.

"You look well ready for action," Orville observed.

"Bush adventure," Viggo confessed sheepishly.

"Why you don't come with me," Orville suggested. "Plenty action up by where I going." The action, he explained, was an old woman who served scraps every evening without as much as a cat to contend with. For Orville, that was action enough.

"I pass by the market yesterday," Orville said as they started along a path Viggo was unfamiliar with.

"I must have been in the gut," Viggo said proudly.

"When I see the alley empty, I think . . ."

"A dog eat me?" Viggo smiled.

"No," Orville answered. "I think maybe you done head up mountain already."

◆

As they moved along the shadowy path, Viggo told Orville about his brush with Hannibal and about the times he'd already spent in the gut. The path took them up and along a ridge and then back into the gut much higher than Viggo had been before. Beyond that, Orville explained, was the last big bend and the edge of town. Viggo could see it was also where the mountain started up. Orville stopped atop a large flat rock.

Above them, limbs of a giant tamarind tree ran like rivers across the twilight sky, converging into a funnel of thick knots on the gut's far side. One of the tree's roots had burst the retaining wall and snaked into the gut where they sat. On the other side of the wall firelight showed beneath the branches. An occasional spark drifted up and went black. Viggo heard voices.

"Now when we go," Orville instructed, "don't move too close to the fire at first."

"Why?"

"Plenty animal does come around here, but I never see the old woman feed a mongoose yet."

"What kind of woman?" Viggo asked.

"Don't worry. Come."

Viggo wondered about the wisdom of getting close to any fire. He followed Orville through a wedge of limb and around the wide, twisted roots of the tree. He hung back in the shadows while Orville moved closer to the fire. There was an old woman and a man and a kettle between them. The man sat on a log, his feet splayed in the fireside dirt, one hand easy on a stone, the other toying with a pipe. He spoke to the woman in a slow, rambling way. She was thin

and dark; wild tufts of hair sprouted flamelike from her head. She used a stick to speak to the fire with pokes and jabs. Viggo watched her pick up a blade and work it through a cassava root, and the veins in her arms danced in the firelight.

"Okay, Callwood," she said, wiping the blade on her hem, "let me see what you bring today."

The man reached behind the log and brought forth a white parcel. "The butcher ain send much today, Manteoba," he said, unwrapping it. Then probing with one finger, he added, "Pig snout, bullfoot, couple fish head . . . and this." He held the piece up as if unsure of its origin.

Manteoba eyed the dangling flesh.

"That belong to a chicken," she said, taking the whole mess and dumping it into the kettle.

The fire licked up and played her shadow against the door of her shack, which Viggo saw for the first time. It was made of goatwood and biscuit tins and was so enmeshed in roots that the huge tree seemed to have burst straight out of it. Manteoba stood up. Her shadow rose up the tree and fell into the night.

"Okay, Mister, time for you," she said, hovering in the vapors and gesturing to one side. There Viggo saw a goat flickering on the edge of the light. The old woman searched the dark waters with her stick and fished out the steaming and discolored remains of the cassava. She laid it on the log beside her and mashed it with a smooth, flat stone.

"What make you think he go eat that?" the man asked.

"He belly paining him," she explained.

She held up the cassava, and out of the darkness came

the head of the goat. He took the cassava and chewed it thoughtfully. Callwood tapped his pipe and used a wooden match to clean the bowl. The goat got down the last of it and let out a long, low baa.

"You can't tell me you feeling better already," Manteoba scolded him gently. "All you ramgoat is some lying rascal. Go chase the ladies, man. Go eat some tin can."

Instead, the goat drew closer and nudged her. Manteoba searched his shoulder and, finding a spot, scooped up some ashes and rubbed them into a sore. The goat stood motionless, his eyes closed. Then a cloud crossed the moon, and a bird sounded on a limb behind Viggo. The old woman turned quickly and spotted him, the light of the fire still in her eyes like twin coals that softened when she saw him. Orville quickly moved to Viggo's side and wagged his tail.

"Come, child. What you hiding so for?" she said, gesturing at Viggo with her stick. "Come for some porridge."

"Must be the dog friend," the man observed with a smile.

"Come, my dumpling," Manteoba urged again, this time putting down her stick. Viggo studied the area around the fire and, with Orville's urging, moved closer, settling in some roots just out of reach.

Callwood shifted his weight and took a long draw on his pipe. "I don't believe I ever see a mongoose looking so well fed," he said, a trail of smoke billowing out of his nostrils.

Manteoba said nothing to this. She filled two small gourds, one for Orville and the other for his friend. Viggo offered her a polite little bow and sat patiently waiting for the brew to cool. It smelled better than it looked, he decided, casting a distrusting look at the lumpy gruel. But the bowl was full and in front of him as sure as the fire. Dutifully he lowered his snout to it and took his first sip.

The potion was strong and true and the goodness spread through him. The man was once again caught up in something and Manteoba pretended to listen. But as the next sip of porridge went down, the old woman caught Viggo's eye and gave him a little wink.

Viggo steadied his bowl and moved closer to her fire.

"Town Bush"

Viggo's evening of firelight was followed by others. Most nights he was there with Orville, the man, and the old woman, but sometimes there were others who came. One was a big yellow dog, a sunny idler he'd seen drift through the market. Then there was a young girl, familiar from somewhere, and a third face that belonged to a ghoulish, long-fingered fellow who sold candles in the shadows of the market. Around the fire this one showed a toothy smile and palmed a congo drum as the kettle boiled.

Viggo enjoyed the food and the warmth of the fire, but he knew the old woman was the real reason he came. The others he recognized by their scent or their sound or by what they wore. But Manteoba carried no scent, except after she'd hugged a goat or used her fingers to wipe a blade.

Her dress had an odor, however, a bewildering scent Orville claimed belonged to another time.

Orville showed Viggo how to measure the evening by the way she prepared her fire. If, early on, she was stumped and silent and fed only twigs to the flames, the night would end early. On the other hand, if she assembled a stack of wood, there was sure to be a blaze and some carrying on. She never said much and seldom appeared to hear what was being said, her mind somewhere lost in the fire. Viggo and Orville spent long hours watching her, trying to unravel what it was in her and in themselves that made them stare. When she stared back, Orville said he thought he knew what she was thinking. Like detectives they assigned significance to everything. Once when she pulled a can out of her sack—so shiny and real and unlike her other belongings—they fixed on it like a clue that could tell them who or what she was.

Time around Manteoba's fire had a calming effect on Viggo. Though he still knew each morning that he'd failed to go up mountain the day before, it seemed to matter less. At least now he stayed away from the market and Hannibal. Instead, he spent his days in the gut with Orville and his nights in the roots of the old woman's tree. His mother's stories of the bush were alive in him once again and he believed, in a way, that he was living such a story, and that the gut was, in a way, like bush. Feelings of mongooseness sometimes moved him to boast about his bush forebears to Orville, his friend and patient listener.

On their walks around the gut, Viggo acquired some of Orville's war-weary gait. The walks took on the urgency of patrols, with Viggo playing scout, practicing again to be brave. He pretended Orville was a beast who depended on his quick moves to ferret out enemies hidden in the bush. It was all make-believe, for sure, but it made Viggo feel brave. And Orville didn't seem to mind playing along.

But one afternoon, on their way to the old woman, they stumbled on a rat nosing through a stump. The creature was so hard at his rooting he didn't hear them approach. Viggo had an easy meal, but he mounted only a modest attack and let the rat escape. He laughed and pretended he wasn't really interested in it. But inside, Viggo was discouraged. His fearless ancestors would have laughed at such cowardice.

That night around the fire he was downcast and without appetite, his porridge grown cold in the bowl. He longed to be a real mongoose living with other mongooses. In a way, the fire that had lured him off the street now made him feel he'd not gone far enough. He sulked in a knuckle of root. His pouting and his untouched bowl had not escaped the old woman's notice.

"But I can't see how they all drown," Callwood said, drawing on his pipe. He was rambling about a schooner that had gone down with all hands. He seemed buoyed by the tragedy and was relishing each detail. He blamed the reef; Manteoba blamed the storm. The captain was blameless because he was a cousin to Callwood. His talk continued, and the old woman picked up a bowl and began to scour it. Viggo watched her powerful hands work circles in the bowl. He was thinking about being brave.

"I can't self kill a rat," he blurted, his worries returned.

"You like to eat rat?" Orville asked, lifting his head off his paws.

"No," Viggo answered.

"So what you want to kill one for?"

"Is so mongoose supposed to be," Viggo said. "My ancestor them was brave brave, you know!"

Orville grunted. He'd grown weary of Viggo's worries and all his talk about ancestors. It was not wrong to live in town; it was not wrong to live in the bush. But to be one thing always wishing to be the other was tiresome. When Orville looked up, he was surprised to find Manteoba staring at him. Her eyes were telling him something.

"I need to get brave to go bush," Viggo said.

"Maybe you need to go bush to get brave instead," Orville replied.

"I been bush already," Viggo answered.

"What bush?"

"All like in the gut."

Manteoba made a sound. Viggo looked up to see her eyes slant over to Orville and into the fire.

"That ain no bush," Orville told him.

"But up by highroad," Viggo persisted, certain Orville was mistaken and that the scrub they'd wandered around in was real bush through and through.

"Town bush," Orville said.

Orville's words and the way he spoke them surprised Viggo. They were measured and slow as if they were rising from an unknown place inside. Orville stared at the old woman and she stared back, the fire still hard in her eyes.

"You like to talk about bush too much, dreaming all the time," the voice went on. "You must be dream town and bush is the same thing."

Viggo mumbled something that Orville, his chin back resting on his paws, didn't hear. Viggo turned to the fire. The man was talking loudly, his finger jabbing the air.

"And not one survive!" Callwood exclaimed, still on the shipwreck. "And is only a short distance they had to swim, man. Now, in my day a seaman could swim. Seem now the onliest thing swimming is fish. In my day a man was a man, man. I don't know what they is today."

"Same thing with mongoose," Manteoba said to the kettle.

"Eh?" Callwood said.

"I say mongoose the same way," she repeated, raising her voice and leveling her stare at Viggo. "Had a day mongoose was mongoose. And bush was bush."

"Oh," Callwood said, still not following but also looking at Viggo. "Uh-huh."

Silence fell, and Viggo felt suddenly awkward and undeserving lounging there in the roots of the big tree. Manteoba looked away, and Callwood picked up where he'd left off. She seemed to be listening. Viggo did a bit of seeming himself, suddenly interested in cleaning his tail. When he heard Orville snoring, he felt he had an excuse to go. There were smiles from the man and woman and no fuss made of his departure. He left the dying light of the fire and slipped away. The gut was dark and the moon had fallen from the sky.

He carried his troubles down the gut and curled up with them on a large boulder beside a quiet pool. He lay at the edge, his dark thoughts over the water. Faraway memories visited him there, things that seemed to have no bearing on matters. He remembered his mother and a bone she once gave him. He remembered a hermit crab moving through the grass and sounds of the market on a day gone by. And beyond them all was an old churchyard memory of mountains and valleys, rising and falling in him like a song.

"A Big Fellow Now"

The next afternoon Viggo caught up with Orville, chewing his foot in the shadows of the bridge. He had made up his mind and was eager to tell his friend, but he was surprised to find that Orville had forgotten their conversation of the night before.

"And you tell me all how I like to dream too much," Viggo reminded him.

Orville stopped chewing his foot and looked into space. "I tell you so?"

"Yes, and you tell me how the gut ain no bush."

Orville scratched his head trying to remember.

"And how only up mountain have real bush," Viggo added, this statement more like a question. Orville didn't remember this either, though the words were certainly true.

"You don't remember?"

"I remember something, yes."

"Well," Viggo announced. "Guess where I going?"

"Where?"

"Up mountain," Viggo said, "all the way in the bush."

Orville had heard this sort of thing before. Still, there was a calm in Viggo's eye.

"When you going?"

"Tonight self," Viggo answered, his brow wrinkled with the thought of it.

"But you ain making joke!"

"I ain making joke, no."

"Good. But watch out. Sometimes when you talk about it too much, it come hard to do," Orville warned.

"I know how you mean," Viggo replied. It reminded him of something else, something Clovis told him. Then, as he reached for the memory, an alien feeling swept over him. What was it? The shadow of a palm moved on the wall and sent a shimmy of fear up his spine. The gut seemed to be wrapping around him, pulling his vision to both sides.

"Viggo," Orville said in a changed voice.

"Eh?" The feeling still wrapped around him.

"Hannibal coming up behind you."

That was it. Some forgotten instinct was sounding an alarm, telling him where danger lurked. Without looking he could feel Hannibal enter the shadow of the bridge. Viggo's chest was tight and his tongue thick in his mouth, and he turned to face the bulldog.

"Only now you turn around?" Hannibal rasped, one tooth poking out his spongy black lips like a tusk. His nostrils flared, and a ribbon of drool slipped down his jowls. He snarled and snapped and backed them both into the rocks.

"Leave him," Orville growled, moving between them.

"Old dog, get from here."

"We got no quarrel with you," Viggo said.

"You forget the stick the marketlady hit me?" Hannibal asked Viggo.

Viggo didn't answer. He saw a bird swoop off a roof and perch on a wire and smelled moss on a nearby rock. He was frightened and outside himself, seeing and feeling everything without taking his eye off the only thing that mattered, the one good eye, the blue one. Hannibal was saying something else, trying to throw them off guard. Then he lunged.

Orville met him halfway but in an instant was a blur beneath Hannibal. Then there was a wild yelp, and Orville shot out to one side. At the same instant Viggo sprang, his instincts aiming him toward the bulldog's throat. But Hannibal reared and Viggo's bite missed, latching onto some useless fat instead. Hannibal stopped and smiled and twisted his neck to bring Viggo up close to the blue eye, wide and bulging. He let out a throaty chuckle and then threw himself into a wild convulsion. Viggo's body flailed like a whip and sailed onto the rocks. His ribs landed hard, and the wind went out of him. Then on the edge of darkness, he saw the bulldog coming to finish him off. In his mind, he knew the end was near.

But his body didn't know. From the animal depth he'd never plumbed, all pain, all fear, all doubt vanished, and for an instant he was mongoose, pure and true. The fulsome bulldog reared in final attack, but Viggo dodged out of his shadow and bolted up the gut like light.

Viggo and Orville retreated to their favorite spot above the gut, the rock face Viggo used for his bush imaginings.

Orville sniffed the air and looked over the roofs of town. Viggo looked out too. He had fought for the first time and survived, but he'd been lucky; he didn't feel like the noble fighter he'd longed to be. There was a cost to the business of being brave. He looked at Orville's shaggy face, at the panting pink tongue part way out of his mouth, and the tired but contented look in his eyes. With each of Orville's breaths Viggo felt his final hour in town drawing to an end.

"Win or lose, I does always feel sick after a fight," Orville said. "To tell the truth, I does feel more sick when I win."

They had talked a long time about the fight and had now almost run out of things to say. A rooster call ricocheted up the valley, leaving a moment of silence behind it. Orville looked at him.

"So, how you feel?"

"Ready," Viggo answered. "A little afraid."

"Don't mind that. From time you start up mountain you go feel better. And when you get high up, you go feel good good again."

Viggo looked at his friend, feeling a little good already.

"And when you get up, don't think you already reach where you looking to go," Orville cautioned. "Go west. It go take time to find real bush."

"I go find it, yes," Viggo replied.

"Good you." Orville measured Viggo with his eyes. Then he stood up, stretched and yawned. Viggo rose and stretched too, but there was no yawn in him.

"You go pass by the old woman on your way?" Orville asked.

"I was going there now."

"Leave some food for me."

"You ain coming?"

Orville shook his head. "I go pass up later," he said. "But I going down the trail now."

Viggo took in the meaning of these words.

"You going down, I going up," he said, looking at his feet.

"You is a big fellow now," Orville told him.

"Is you help me," Viggo replied.

"Take care yourself, and if you meet a rooster, send word."

"I go send it, yes," Viggo promised.

"Okay then."

"All right."

"All right then."

"Okay."

Then they turned and walked their separate ways.

Into the Darkness

It was still early when he got to the bend. Blue showed through the limbs above him, distant tributaries of the trunk that grew beside her fire. He would wait until he saw firelight or heard voices. But he was impatient, ready to be away from the place. His thoughts followed the wind's upward curve across the slope, and in the drifting calm he closed his eyes and tried to imagine the mountain. The instant his thoughts reached out, he heard her voice. He scrambled down the bank, crossed the gut, and climbed the wall on the other side.

"See you there," Manteoba said, standing beside her shack, a bundle of twigs in one hand and strands of guinea grass in the other. "Come sit here and let me tie up these stick." She patted a place on the log to show her meaning.

He sat on her log and watched her sort and tie. She talked and he listened, trying to make sense of her sounds. He felt strange to be there before she'd started the fire, and to help fill the time he became interested in the bundles she was tying. She watched him from the corner of her eye. When she rose to shake out a rag, Viggo studied her grace as she moved from the kettle to the pail, from the pail to the log.

"You well still this afternoon," she said, sitting back beside him. Then she pointed through the limbs of the tree to the mountain beyond and asked him something.

Viggo looked where she pointed.

"When I was a girl—a long time ago, mind—the mountain was my home." Here she closed her eyes. "It had a road going up, a winding dirt road. I used to live to the very very end."

Viggo loved the sound of her voice. Though he understood nothing, her sounds made him think of a young girl walking a country lane, trailing a stick. There was a dog walking with the girl and a dense green tangle of bush behind. This was where he would go.

The old woman was drawing in the dirt with her stick, pointing at her lines and telling him with slow words and unblinking eyes more things he couldn't understand.

"Is a valley near to the sea with fruit tree growing and fresh breeze blowing. Keep the wind to you back, and you sure to find it—bush and the way thing use to be."

Viggo was looking at her, thinking about the mountain and the steep green promise of its slopes. It would be sad leaving her, going only to go without knowing where. He looked at the deep lines in her neck. She seemed older in the daylight. What would become of her? he wondered.

"And don't worry about me," she said. "I been here long time, child, and I ain going nowhere."

The stick she gestured with pointed at Viggo, and he noticed a slight quiver in her hand. She put the stick down as if she'd noticed the same thing, then rose and shook out her skirt as if to shoo something away. In the tree a bird sounded. It wasn't a thrush. The call was unfamiliar to Viggo. The sound was answered from a tree farther up; then a volley of song went from limb to limb, higher and higher above.

"Mountain dove," Manteoba said.

Wind gusted through the tamarind's top, and the creak of a limb vibrated through the air. They both looked up and saw a single leaf falling, wafting down in arcs and settling in the dust beside them. Manteoba scooped Viggo up and held him, warm and woolly, to her old bony breast. Then, in another tongue she sang him a song, and he wished her tune would never die.

"Before you go," she said, putting him down, "come help me light this old fire of mine."

She reached for a long wooden match and struck it. She put it to the twigs, and the flames caught and spread. From where Viggo stood, the brambles of her hair fused with the

gnarly bark of the tree so that the tree seemed to grow right out of her, its wild arms dancing at the sky. They looked at each other for the last time. Fire showed in her eyes, and the magic of the flames passed from her eyes to his. He turned and ran into the bushes.

He was weak from good-byes, tired of being brave. A stream of water in the gut told him that somewhere it was raining. If the sky was not too big for it, he figured, then neither was he. And heavy of heart, making his way up the gut, he cried.

He followed the gut until he was forced to pick his way through the underbush bit by bit. After some time the bushes broke onto a switchback where the road turned on itself, making its way up. He pressed on and just before nightfall came to a deep notch where the road passed from one side of the mountain to the other. He stopped there, stunned to see how high he'd climbed and how fast. On one side was town, distant and doll-like, its lights still working their enchantment, and on the other side was only darkness, waiting.

He perched himself on a stone and watched the sun slide into the sea. Then, summoning his courage, he continued around the bend and into the darkness. When town's lights had faded fully from sight, he groped a bit farther, climbed a bank above the road, and felt out a place in the roots of a tree.

He fought off sleep for a while by holding fast to the light of a star. But the star soon closed his eyes. His sleep was deep and his dreams sturdy and stout-hearted, readying him to wake in a new land.

Part Two

Drake's Seat

Viggo woke at sunrise, his senses startled by the high light, the silence and the cool air. He felt like a visitor in his own body, staring out of it for the first time.

He rose and climbed a slope until he could see over the trees. The mountain beneath him was a random tumble of haystack hills stampeding to the coast. No roofs rose out of it, and no roads carved it into parts. To the east a velvety chain of islands cast long shadows across the water. It wasn't water like the polished swirls he'd known in town. Here it was dark and deep, swells rolling to shore, climbing the plunging cliffs. He held himself still to preserve the moment, but a thrush squawked indifferently from a nearby limb.

He scratched the crumbs of earth from his fur and then stretched. His sore haunches stirred memories of his long climb. He was hungry. He picked up a hog plum seed and chewed it, trying to see his way to his first meal. He looked west to the land that lay before him, each lovely hill a sobering repetition of the one before. He sank back on his haunches feeling unequal to the task.

The sudden straining of an engine broke the silence.

The lazy morning of birdsong had led him to believe he'd left this sort of thing behind. But a gaily painted safari tour bus rolled by below him and came to a stop around the corner. Viggo streaked through the trees for a closer look.

At a widening in the road a cargo of fleshy sightseers poured out of the bus in hats and sandals, swinging cameras and shopping bags. The driver's bullhorn directed their attention to the spectacular view and to a donkey. For a small fee, the bullhorn informed them, they could sit on the beast and have their photos taken. The donkey was tied to a tree.

The driver hefted several large ladies onto the donkey's back. Viggo watched through the bushes, trying to sort out the mysterious ritual. Throughout the ordeal, the donkey, who wore a straw hat embellished with bougainvillea, maintained a dignified expression unlike that of the donkeys he'd seen in town. Soon the sightseers were back on board, and the bus continued down the road.

So far, Viggo observed, the mountain was not so different from town.

When the bus was out of earshot, he went closer, determined to strike up a conversation with the donkey and learn a thing or two about the road. He also had a mind to peek in the trashcan to see if the people had left any food behind. The donkey was dozing. Viggo stood on the wall just below his big fuzzy nose. His huge gray head was framed by flowers, but his eye showed a trail worn by tears. Viggo wondered how best to arouse him.

"Nice view," he said cheerfully.

The donkey jolted awake. Then, seeing his visitor was

not a tourist, the alert look soured to one of disdain. He eyed Viggo as one might eye a thief, his nose crinkled as if in the company of an offensive odor. He said nothing.

"Nice view," Viggo tried again.

The animal seemed determined to ignore him. He looked out at the view with sudden interest as if something new had caught his attention. Then he looked at the wind in the tree as if that too were an uncommon curiosity. Viggo looked out too. He hadn't expected the donkey to be rude, and he wondered whether it was worth the effort. He looked at the trashcan, but it was empty. Then he had an idea. He went over the wall and yanked up a clump of guinea grass and toyed with it beneath the donkey's nose.

"This is your home?" he asked.

The donkey reacted to the question as if it were a piece of rudeness. But the scent of the fresh grass began to get the better of him.

"You can't see where you standing up?" the donkey replied in a haughty undonkeylike way. "This is Drake Seat, the most beautifullest view in the world. The people them come from all over the place to look this. They like the view and they love me. I does come from a long line of famous jackass."

"That's nice," Viggo said, handing him some grass. "What your name is?"

"Funky," the donkey answered.

"That's a nice name," Viggo said, twiddling the grass.

"That's my tourist name," the donkey explained. "My real name is *Equus asinus,* of course."

"Oh," Viggo said, handing him the rest.

"Just like yours own is *Herpestes auropunctatus auro-punctatus,*" he added with his mouth full.

"My name is Viggo," Viggo said, certain the donkey had mistaken him for someone else.

"That's your given name, stupid," the donkey replied, swallowing a wad of weeds. "Herpestes is your real name. Like *E pluribus unum* and all them thing."

"Them is some big word," Viggo said, a bit confused.

"Well, you could just call me Funky," the donkey said with a generous nod. "That grass taste sweet sweet, eh?" he added, angling for another clump.

Viggo went over the wall to wrestle with some fresh shoots. He hoped the donkey would tell him about the road and the quickest way to the bush.

"You does know this road?" he asked, watching still more grass disappear into the donkey's face.

"Maybe," the donkey replied. "What part you looking to go?"

"I looking to go so," Viggo said, pointing west.

The donkey frowned. "If is the hotel you looking to go, don't bother. The view ain no better than right here and the place full of rat. A dog tell me is a rodent heaven up there."

"I going to the bush," Viggo explained.

"The *bush!*" the donkey exclaimed. "Ha!"

"What so funny?"

"The bush a long way from here."

"For true?"

"And most mongoose prefer a good can of garbage, anyhow. Ain got no garbage in the bush," he warned.

"But that's why I going there," Viggo said.

"You go be sorry."

Viggo thought about this a moment.

"It have guinea grass in the bush," he said. "If you was free you could eat it all day."

"Free? I done free already!" the donkey protested. "I get plenty food, and the tourist them does feed me too. Mongoose can't tell me about being free."

A gust of wind lifted the flowers, and Viggo saw the raw flesh where the rope dug in. The flies were having a go at it.

"You want me try loose the rope so it don't hurt so bad?" Viggo offered.

"This rope don't hurt," the donkey assured him. "You couldn't loose it anyway. It strong strong." He gave it a tug with his teeth, proud of the sureness of the knot.

The sound of an engine finding its way around the hill faded in and out of the valley.

"Big Time," the donkey said, his frown replaced by a smile.

"Big Time?" Viggo asked.

"Big Time," the donkey repeated. "That's what I call the driver of the pink and white. He right on schedule. You best move from here, though. The tourist them don't like mongoose like they love donkey."

"Oh," Viggo said with a worried look.

"But if you stick around," the donkey said, "it might have some garbage when they gone."

"No thanks," Viggo said. He spotted the pink and white rounding the bend, trailing a film of blue exhaust.

"Good luck, Funky," he said, turning to go.

But the donkey didn't hear. His tail was busy batting flies, his head eagerly awaiting the next load.

Prosper

It troubled Viggo that his first encounter with a mountain animal had been so unfriendly, but he trusted that creatures farther down the road would be wilder. He imagined what it would be like to see his first mongoose and even wondered if the bush might hold some new and unexpected creature.

For several hours he followed the road west. Along the way there were sights and sounds that were new and wonderful to him. The road narrowed and the trees grew taller and a canopy of shadows unfurled about him. He found pleasure in this. It was as he'd imagined it when Clovis once spoke of his early goat days in the country. But as the sun climbed higher and the shadows shrank back and the road grew hot, he began to wonder if the road was taking him where he wanted to go or playing him a trick. Twice it forked, and both times he chose the steeper, more troubling way, hoping to rise out of the trees and be able to see where he was. He was hungry and tired, and his noble thoughts about life in the wild were beginning to unravel. He stopped noticing the trees and the sweet birdsongs and began thinking about what he'd give for a bowl of Manteoba's stew or one of Ziggy's dumplings.

"It ain got no garbarge in the bush," he said aloud,

repeating the donkey's warning. If there wasn't any garbage there certainly wouldn't be any stew; and dumplings, he knew, did not grow on trees. Slowly, the thought of turning back began to creep into his mind.

But finally the road widened, and the tangled bushes gave way to a neat row of palms, flowery shrubs, and a mango tree. Nearby, a driveway curved down to a large red roof. At the head of the drive was a low wall with a ceramic basin—a birdbath, judging from the droppings—and next to it a handsome red, white, and blue mailbox with the name MRS. GERTRUDE HORNBLOWER LONGBOTTOM emblazoned in gold letters upon it. After drinking from the basin, Viggo rested in the undulating shadows of the palms and went to work on a fallen mango. He was feeling much restored. In minutes his muzzle and paws were coated with the juicy orange pulp.

His sumptuous luncheon was not going unnoticed. A dog in the shadows of the hibiscus was studying him with keen interest. A mongoose in this neighborhood was rare enough, but this one was particularly noteworthy. Most mongooses kept to the high grass and seldom showed a whisker. This one had marched right up the road, helped himself to the basin water, and now, without regard for private property, was lunching on the dog's wall. He had half a mind to scare him off. But the mongoose had piqued his curiosity.

The dog strolled onto the road, pretending not to notice Viggo, and began to scratch. Viggo looked up from his mango and saw through the dog's show. He eyed him narrowly, sizing up the threat. He seemed tame enough,

Viggo figured, and maybe he could tell him about the fork in the road just ahead.

"Good day," Viggo said, rising on his hind legs. "You live round here?"

"Yes," the dog answered, startled to be addressed by a mongoose. "That's my house down there."

"You know what part these road does go?" Viggo asked, pointing to the junction ahead. The question produced a smile in the corner of the dog's mouth, as if it told the dog something the dog wanted to know.

"Depends which way you're going," the dog responded.

"I going down so," Viggo said, pointing west.

"Both roads go down," the dog began. "The left one goes down, across, up, and around, and the right one goes up, around, across, and down." The dog paused to allow time for the confusion to sink in. "Then this across and down comes into that up and around on the other side. Got that?"

"Uh-huh," Viggo mumbled. He noticed the dog had a strange accent.

"Then you come to a confusing junction called Four Corners where a missed turn could lead to dire consequences."

"What kind of place that is?" Viggo asked.

"What kind of place is what?"

"Drier how-it-name."

The dog took a long second look at Viggo and raised an eyebrow.

"You don't look like the down type," the dog remarked. "How far down are you wanting to go?"

"All the way in the bush," Viggo answered.

"That's through farmland," the dog cautioned. "You ever been to this bush before?"

Viggo shook his head.

"I see." The dog looked at Viggo and then at the sky. "Look, it's still early. I know a place where you can at least see where you're going. It's not far from here."

Viggo looked up the road.

"I mean I can accompany you," the dog explained. "I'm always up for a romp, and there's a certain dog and a rock thrower I can help you with."

"That would be very kind of you," Viggo replied.

"My name is Prosper."

"Pleasing to make the pleasure," Viggo said politely. "Mines own is Viggo."

He rinsed his paws and face in the birdbath and Prosper lifted his leg at the mailbox, and the two of them started up the road.

Prosper was an average dog (except for his rhinestone collar) with a lopsided look about him. His fur was spotted black and white except for a rear paw that appeared to wear an orange sock. One ear aspired to stand up but collapsed halfway from the effort, while the other was white and floppy. He had a dashing black ring around his right eye and a shocking pink tongue hanging from the left side of his mouth. His nose was invisibly connected to his tail in a way that caused one to go up when the other went down. He had it easy compared to any dog Viggo had known in town.

"I've been in the service of Mistress Longbottom my entire life," he said with a note of pride. "My grandfather was her puppy when she was a child. He was a German shepherd."

"Oh," Viggo said with big eyes, not understanding but sensing this was a thing of some importance to Prosper.

"So, I'm your average north-side bowser. I do a bit of barking and growling and get my share of chicken liver and horsemeat."

"That sound good," Viggo said.

"I also get a bone on my birthday or when I uncover something special with my nose. That's the beagle in me. I've got a very talented nose."

"It look so," Viggo said, walking beside him.

Prosper guided Viggo through a residential area, past stately entrances, iron gates, terraced gardens, and more mailboxes and barking dogs, to a small park high on the hill. There they went to a promontory of boulders where Viggo could see what lay before him. The land traveled west in an unblemished procession of green hills. Clouds towered above the bowed line of the horizon, and a lace of shoals skirted the coast. Viggo was touched by the sight and by the bending grass and deepening sky.

"I come here a lot," Prosper said. "Just to look."

"You don't never want to go?" Viggo asked.

"Oh, it's not as pretty as it looks," Prosper said without a moment's thought. "Much of what you see is farmland and bush—creatures fighting to survive. I have to endure a lot of fussing and flea powder, but at least I know where my next meal is coming from."

"I know how you mean," Viggo said.

"And I can always wander up here to look," Prosper added. "But in a way this view is like a scenic painting my mistress has on the dining room wall. It's nice to look at, but in the end it's just a picture. Know what I mean?"

"Uh-huh," Viggo answered, not knowing at all. Prosper seemed to know a great deal more than the donkey about where Viggo was going, but it was hard to believe something so pretty could be as dangerous as he made it sound.

"You should consider staying around here," Prosper suggested. "This is both bush and prime garbage-belt territory. The scraps are fantastic. It won't be so easy after Four Corners."

"What that is?" Viggo asked.

"The next junction. After that it's unknown territory—no garbage, maybe no water, farmers with traps and guns."

Viggo watched Prosper's face grow worried with wrinkles, as if he were trying to untangle the snarled tendrils of the ketch-an-keep bush in front of him.

"Maybe I best stay the night here," Viggo murmured.

"A wise decision," Prosper said, nodding his head.

Then to further dampen Viggo's interest in the bush, Prosper went on to describe the many dangers he'd heard about from animals who'd been there and lived to tell the story.

"If I was going that way, there are a number of things I'd be asking myself," Prosper started.

"Thing like what?"

"What if I got hit by a car, for instance? Or what if I got shot by a farmer or caught and tied up? And what if I wanted to come back home but my mistress wouldn't let me in?"

The what-ifs continued one after another, much to Viggo's distress. Prosper seemed to enjoy these bouts of speculation and relished the effect they had on Viggo.

"And be on the lookout for wizards," he advised. "You know about wizards, of course?"

"That's something like a lizard?" Viggo asked.

"Heavens no!" Prosper exclaimed. "A wizard is . . . is a magical trickster."

"What they does look like?"

"A wizard looks like whatever a wizard wants to look like," Prosper informed him in a whisper, as if one might be looking over their shoulders at that moment. "Some look like two-headed monsters, others like animal-eating trees."

"For true?" Viggo asked wide-eyed.

Prosper made a face. "Squeeze the life right out of you."

Viggo swallowed a large lump that had gathered in his throat.

"If you decide the bush isn't worth the risks," Prosper concluded, "you know where I live. I'll give you a tour of the neighborhood garbage cans, and you'll not be disappointed."

"You very kind," Viggo said.

"Now," Prosper said, rising, "you'll have to excuse me. Much as the view appeals to my wanderlust, this time of day appeals to a baser instinct, my appetite."

"Maybe I go see you tomorrow," Viggo heard himself say.

"First thing in the morning," Prosper replied as if it was a sure thing. "I'll show you a garbage can or two." With that he turned and started down the hill. Viggo watched his tail and bobbing rump disappear behind a knob of turf, retreating to the wonders of his dog bowl.

With Prosper gone, the seed of what he'd said rooted itself inside Viggo, and his fear began to grow. Perhaps Prosper was right; perhaps this was already bush and Viggo hadn't realized it. He looked up at a tree and imagined it coming to life and swallowing him whole.

"But see how that dog got me thinking," he scolded aloud.

He picked himself up and walked around in the remaining light, brushing his fears aside. Twilight had begun to descend like a silent curtain, pressing down on the horizon's thin violet line. He grew less concerned with what lay beyond the bend and concentrated on smaller things instead—a beetle, cobwebs, blades of grass.

One plant reminded him of one that grew by the churchyard gate where he used to wait for his mother to return from her shantytown wanderings. He thought of her and of the stories she told, and in a strange way he felt she was near. He saw a snail making its way through the grass and pretended she was there, over his shoulder, telling him to look. Later, when night had come, crickets and tree frogs serenaded him and brought to mind a lullaby his mother once sang. The music was still strong inside him; it seemed to grow, vibrating, out of the earth. He remembered the song, the starlight, Clovis and the other goats, and his mind again reached back to the stories of long ago.

If so much had happened to him in so short a time, Viggo thought, who could predict what awaited him in the days and weeks ahead, in the valleys and ridges of the land that lay to the west? He looked up at the stars as if they could provide an answer. They were clearer and closer on the mountain than they were in town, keener, more interested observers.

But they only blinked at Viggo's wonderings, wise but far, and offered him no clues.

Rupert

Viggo was up at dawn. Before he set off, he went to the big blue rock he and Prosper had stood on and left a flower weighted down by a stone.

As he started out, he noticed his limbs were not as tender as the day before; already he'd been hardened by the climb. Overnight he'd shed much of the fear Prosper had intended to inspire. He felt puffed up with the promise of the day and was certain the world meant him well. At each turn in the road he felt he knew something of what lay on the other side. He imagined that this was the bush awakening in him.

But around one bend he discovered something he had not expected—a green, boxlike thing notched into the side of the hill. As he drew closer, he saw it was a garbage bin with bright flowers and birds painted on its side. It was the very prettiest bin he'd ever seen, though the smell was not much prettier than bins he's smelled in town. As he drew closer, he heard a wild, swarming commotion coming from inside.

Then, out of the bin popped a mongoose! Viggo watched in stunned silence, scarcely believing the creature was one of his own. He looked dirty and desperate and mean—his teeth tearing into a fuzzy piece of flesh, a mad, red look in his eyes. Viggo decided not to introduce himself and slipped into the high grass on the far side of the road. When he got a little downwind, a horrible stench overwhelmed him. He looked back. Between the bin and the edge of the road he spotted the bloated body of a dead cat, its four legs sticking straight up at the sky.

An hour west, after several soothing green bends in the road, Viggo came to a place where the road crossed the spine of the mountain. Through the trees he caught a glimpse of town far to the east, glistening in the morning light. The lines that crisscrossed it were the streets he had known, with less meaning to him now than the nearest tree. Was this the last he'd see of it? he wondered. He stayed a moment, thinking about all he was leaving behind and the many unknowns that awaited him around the bend.

From there the road nudged higher into a bamboo thicket and down to a saddle in the mountain where four roads converged. This, Viggo figured, was the Four Corners Prosper had spoken of. Approaching it, he spotted an old man and a goat standing in the shadows of a tree. The man appeared to be talking to the goat. Viggo was heartened. A goat was always a good sign. He continued straight toward them on his hind legs.

"But see how this mongoose coming up the road!" the man exclaimed. "He well bold."

Viggo came right up beside them.

The old man wore frayed and baggy pants, suspenders, and a cap.

"Good day to you, young fellow," he said with a slight bow, "Leviticus Webster at your service."

He smiled, and Viggo saw a silver star on his front tooth.

"I don't know who teach you walk down the road like that," he warned, "but round here you best stay low, else you go catch a shot."

The man scratched the goat's head, and Viggo wondered what he had said. The goat nodded and the man nodded and the two closed their eyes.

"Best go before the road get too hot," the man said. He gave the goat a parting salute and hoisted a large sack onto his shoulder. Viggo and the goat watched him start down, moving in and out of the shadows by the side of the road.

"That's a big sack," Viggo said.

"He's a coalman," the goat explained. "He taking he charcoal to market to bring back meat from the butcher."

"Meat from who?"

"The butcher. The fellow who does make goat into mutton and pig into pork," the goat replied. "Some of my best friend end up with him."

"I sorry to hear that," Viggo said, hoping he hadn't helped eat any of the goat's friends.

"For what? Around here, don't mind who you is—fowl, pig, goat, cow—you all waiting for the same day."

Viggo was glad not to hear mongoose on the list.

"Car coming," the goat said, sauntering into a blind of

tall grass. Viggo followed, crouched down beside him, and listened to the engine groan closer. He noticed a scar running along the goat's shank and a vein pulsing in his shoulder. Not since Clovis had he been so close to the good smell of a goat. A farm truck rolled past them.

"My name is Rupert," the goat said, moving back to the road.

"Mines own is Viggo."

"You does live round here?" Rupert asked with a puzzled look. Mongooses seldom had much to say to goats.

"I come up from town," Viggo replied.

"From town?" Rupert smiled. "It have mongoose living there?"

"Not too much."

"So where you going?"

"I going down so," Viggo said, pointing west.

"Down where?"

"To the end of the road."

"End of what road?" the goat asked.

Viggo searched for something more definite. His mind settled on a familiar tangle of green.

"I going all the way in the bush," he declared, rising on his hind legs.

"Oh, you going bush," Rupert said, sizing Viggo up. "That's good, but the bush a big place. What part the bush you looking to go?"

Viggo knew the bush was big. He just hadn't thought of going to a particular part of it. He'd imagined it as he'd imagined it, as just one place. Come to think of it, he hadn't given it much thought at all.

"I want to go where the mongoose them running wild," he said at last.

"Then you must be want to go where I going," the goat said.

"Where?"

"Bordeaux. Where the coalman make the charcoal."

"It have mongoose there?"

"Plenty mongoose. And plenty bush too."

Viggo looked down the road.

"It far?" he asked.

"Far for a mongoose," the goat allowed.

"You does have to be brave?" Viggo asked.

Rupert smiled. "No. Long as you really want to get there. But you have to pass through the farms," he warned. "Around there they use animal for labor or fatten them for the dinner table."

Viggo thought about this. He couldn't be made to work—that was for donkeys. He tried to imagine himself simmering in a stew.

"Farmer does eat mongoose?" he asked.

"I don't believe so. But if they catch you meddling in the hen house, they go drive you a shot, kill you dead."

This was beginning to sound more like the bush Prosper had talked about. Was the adventure worth the risks? Viggo thought about the good pickings in the garbage belt.

"Maybe I should stay around here," he said.

"Maybe so."

"And maybe not," he tested the goat.

"Maybe not, yeah," Rupert replied. "I think you go like the bush better. Don't mind it hard to get there. I go show you the way."

"To the end of the road?"

"And the bush beyond."

"How long to get there?"

"Couple day," Rupert replied. "We follow this road. Where the road west turn back east it have a mailbox tree. The trail to Bordeaux start there."

"A mailbox tree?"

"A tree with mailbox on it," Rupert said, pointing to a crooked line of mailboxes where the road forked.

Viggo looked down the road again. Morning light showed around the first bend.

"I only have to make one stop along the way," the goat added.

"What kind of stop?"

"A rooster friend I have to see. No big thing," Rupert assured him. "But see the sun getting high. Come go with me, I go tell you as we walk along."

Crab and Stone

The more Viggo talked with Rupert, the more he was reminded of Clovis. Both had been born wild, captured, and brought west in a truck. Rupert wasn't as old a goat as Clovis, or as big—though he had a handsome and powerful set of horns. In Viggo's eyes the two shared a special goatness, a way with the land and a way of drawing him in with their eyes.

Once west of Four Corners, Viggo felt the presence of

man more strongly. There was the sound of chopping and the haze of brushfire smoke. Tin roofs dotted the hillside, and the road's ruts spoke of wagons and trucks. A certain symmetry pleased the eye: terraced slopes made a staircase to the sea; rows of vegetables hugged the contoured land; patches of banana leaf obeyed the wind. Viggo moved half in fear, half in awe of the place.

With Rupert's help they wound their way through the habitations with little difficulty—forced to jump off the road only once by a passing truck. Twice they stopped to observe people at a distance: a woman mending a terrace and, later, a man tending a fire. Beside one house Viggo spotted a truck he recognized from the market.

Rupert explained that the stop he had to make the next day involved freeing a rooster in distress. The rooster's name was Poncho, and helping him escape would settle a score with a certain cruel farmer. But it required the risky business of returning to the very farm Rupert had escaped from. It didn't sound like a good idea to Viggo and he said so.

"But you don't have to worry," the goat assured him. "Just stay by the road until I bust him out."

"But what if the farmer . . . ?"

"Don't study he. If he look to humbug me, I go give him same thing what I give him last time," Rupert said with a toss of his horns.

Viggo looked at a tree they were passing. It was leaning away from the road, two huge limbs lopped off at the elbow, its trunk girded with barbed wire.

"You butt him?"

"Knock him down."

"Then you run off?"

"No, he already had the rope on me. He tie me by the road for the truck come carry me town. I struggle hard hard to get away, but I get tangle in the fence. When the coalman pass, he meet me there bawling out. Is he set me free."

"He ain look to eat you?"

"No, the coalman is a good fellow; him and me is friend. Is he carry me Bordeaux and is he give me this bell."

Rupert shook his head and the bell jumped up and down.

"It don't ring?" Viggo asked.

"He fix it so if a man see me on the road, he go think I is a farmerman own. But if one of them look to hold me, I could run hide and it won't ring."

"Oh," Viggo said.

"If it wasn't for the coalman, someone would of make mutton of me long time ago."

They selected a culvert with a good view to all sides as a safe place to spend the night. There was water, a soft embankment, and food enough for them both. With a bellyful of papaya and the scent of soursop in the air, Viggo took in the long shadows and deep greens of the cultivated valley. The water gurgling in the culvert seemed like an old friend. For all of its dangers, the farmland appeared to have its rewards.

They traded stories—Rupert about the east end and his life on a farm, and Viggo about the churchyard and town. When Viggo asked Rupert about Bordeaux, he found the goat reluctant to say too much, as if talking about the valley might somehow lessen it. It was green and near to the sea, he told Viggo. There were mongooses and fruit trees. But that is all Viggo learned.

"You go see what you go see," Rupert said.

Still, Viggo trusted him. He believed it would be green and wild and where he wanted to be. He was trying to make a picture of it in his mind when he heard a rustling sound in the grass. Out of it appeared a hermit crab toting his shell. He bumped into a stone, got detoured by a root, and tumbled sideways into the gully beside them.

Rupert smiled at this. "That shell come all the way from the sea," he said.

"I wonder where he going?" Viggo asked.

"He must be wonder the same thing."

Viggo studied the shell's bumbling progress, and it saddened him. He saw in it some of his own groping through the mountain to a place he'd never been.

"I feel for him," he said.

"No sense feeling for a hermit crab," Rupert said. "They ain need it." Then he stared at Viggo, his goat eyes searching something out.

"You ever hear stone?" he asked.

"If I ever hear . . . ?"

"Stone," the goat repeated. "A kind of sound does come out the ground."

Viggo shook his head.

"Hermit crab does hear it all the time," Rupert said.

"They *hear* stone?"

"They is the onliest creature could hear it, because the shell close close to the ground."

Viggo looked dumbly at the stone beneath him.

"It have something to hear?" he asked.

"So they say."

"You ever hear it?"

"Sometime when I waking up I feel like I does hear something, yes. Maybe is something else. But the hermit crab does hear it all the time turning round and round in he shell."

"Who tell you so?" Viggo asked.

Rupert thought a moment. "I think is my mother tell me. And I believe it."

Viggo went over to the crab for a closer look. The hermit's house was an old whelk shell, speckled black and white and faded from the sun. The crab's hard purple legs carried it aloft, while two claws, like armored clamps, led the way. That the shell had once lived beneath the waves was a thing of wonder to Viggo. He remembered the hermit crab Clovis had shown so much interest in.

"Goat like hermit crab a lot, ain't it?" he asked.

Rupert nodded. "We like how they go up a hill."

"Bumping into thing all the time?"

"They get where they going, though," Rupert said. "No mind how rugged it is, hermit crab still ready to climb. Goat something the same way. Don't mind what the road got waiting for you. Just enjoy it as you go along."

The words were similar to ones Clovis had spoken, and they had a clear, true ring to them. For a goat they were a good guide, Viggo decided, but he was a mongoose, and he wanted very much to know what the road had in store. He doubted the words were meant for him.

Rupert drew Viggo's attention to the moon rising out

of the trees. They watched it steal from cloud to cloud, its features concealed.

"What you think that is?"

"The moon?"

Rupert nodded. It seemed like a strange question to Viggo, though he had himself wondered about the moon— about the way it changed shapes and the way it floated across the sky.

"I think maybe is a hole in the night," Rupert said, the white of his coat aglow with it.

Viggo thought about this.

"Maybe is the sun sleeping," he said.

"The sun sleeping," Rupert repeated. "I like that one. You know, sometime mongoose does think something like goat."

"For true?"

"For true. They wonder."

For a moment the crickets stopped, and they both noticed the thin echo of distant waves crashing on a shore far below them.

"When I was a young fellow like you, living in the bush by the sea, I used to wonder a good bit," Rupert mused.

"About what?"

"Stone, moon, tree—all kind of foolishness." A smile crossed his face. "I even use to ask the lizard them tell me what tree does talk about."

"What they tell you?"

"They tell me go ask the wind," Rupert said, shaking his head. "You should of see me standing up talking to the sea breeze."

Viggo studied Rupert. His new goat friend certainly wondered about a lot of strange things.

"I used to try hearing rockstone too."

"For true?"

"All the time."

"And you ain never hear it?" Viggo asked.

Rupert shook his head. "When wave hit cliff, I had think the sound was like what the hermit crab hear. But now I know it ain the stone making the sound, is the water. Like the wave them telling the stone something."

"I know how you mean," Viggo said.

"So I ask a seagull friend tell me what the wave say. He watch me hard, then fly away. Is the onliest thing he ain want to tell me."

"Maybe he ain self know."

"Could be," Rupert nodded. "I know it ain wave alone I ain understand. Wave, wind, tree, stone—they all a mystery to me. But I don't mind. I like to wonder."

Here he paused and looked out into the night.

"And I still believe these trees talking over our head right now," he added.

"Talking?" Viggo asked, peering into the branches.

"In their way."

In the darkness they listened. But Viggo heard only crickets and toads, a far dog, and, in the limbs above, a breath of wind passing.

The Farmerman

On their way west, Rupert told Viggo all about Poncho, the rooster friend he hoped to rescue. Once Poncho had been allowed to run wild and roost in trees. He was everything a good cock should be: proud, smooth with the hens, and quick with a flattering word. But on Rupert's last visit he found the coop almost empty and learned that all but three hens had been taken to market. For the first time the farmer had locked Poncho in the coop and now expected him and the remaining hens to repopulate the coop and provide fresh eggs. But the hens were upset and showed no interest in Poncho's advances or in laying eggs.

Poncho was in a state because the farmer was as impatient as he was cruel. And word of Poncho's problem was getting around. Rodents taunted him with jokes, thrushes peppered him with insults from the papaya tree, and the family tomcat, who was hungry for fowl, gloated from the top of the rain barrel. But this abuse was nothing compared to the farmer's daily machete-sharpening display meant to remind Poncho that, though the farmer preferred a fat hen, he was not opposed to putting a rooster's head on the chopping block—a hideous, stained stump by the chicken coop door.

Rupert told Viggo he'd urged Poncho not to worry. But this advice had led Poncho to worry about worrying, and that in turn had caused further worries about not worrying about worrying. When Rupert last saw Poncho, he was wildly fretting in circles.

♦

They arrived at the dirt turnoff for the farmer's plot late in the afternoon. The turn was marked by the charred stump of a fallen tree and bordered by barbed wire. Rupert showed Viggo a niche in a stone wall where he could wait. But being left alone was beginning to appeal to Viggo even less than going to the coop.

"Maybe I best go with you," Viggo suggested.

"If you want."

"What about the farmer?"

"He does only check the coop in the morning," Rupert replied. "But I know he want to make stew with me. So if you come, you could help watch for him."

Viggo looked down the rutted dirt track. The slithering imprint of a tire wound along it like the skin of a snake, and a frightening picture of what might lurk around the corner flashed across his mind. Rupert was waiting for him to decide. The thistles in his beard, the scar across his shank, and the business end of his horns seemed to be telling Viggo something. Rupert's surefooted shadow started down the road, his hooves digging into the snaking tire track.

"I coming with you," Viggo said, scooting after him.

The coop was notched into the side of the hill, slapped together with chicken wire, galvanized bits, and scraps of wood. The roof was low and the insides dark, and an airless stench hovered around it. Between the hill and the back of the coop was an overgrown crawlspace littered with farm-yard debris. On one side was a wooden spool, a broken plow handle, a rain barrel, and an engine sprouting weeds.

Against the backside of the coop was a crate of egg cartons, a bald tire, a rusted-out wheelbarrow, and a stack of empty cans.

They picked their way through the clutter, careful not to trigger a landslide. There was quiet cooing and clucking inside the coop. Viggo climbed the crate of egg cartons, and Rupert steadied himself on the old tire, and they both pressed their whiskers to the chicken wire.

What they saw was not the picture of a rooster in distress. Poncho was puffed up and strutting on a plank in front of three appreciative and gently clucking hens. He was brown and gold, wrinkled around the feet and eyes but still sporting a rigid red comb.

"Poncho," Rupert whispered through the chicken wire.

Poncho stopped in mid-strut. "Rupert!" the rooster squawked, flapping over to him. "What you doing here?"

"We come to set you free."

"You bring *mongoose* to rescue rooster? You crazy for true."

"Viggo's a friend," Rupert assured him. "He go help get you out."

"It only have one problem," Poncho said with a guilty look.

"What kind of problem?"

"I ain want to get out," the rooster explained.

"But you ain say . . . ?"

"I know what I say, Rupert, but thing better now. They ain henpecking me so bad no more." Here he lowered his voice. "See the one there with the white tail feather? Life in here ain so bad, you know."

"What stupidness you talking?" Rupert replied. "Poncho, in here smell stinks."

"But after a while you don't self notice it," the rooster argued. "And what I go do in the bush? Eat worm? The farmerman feeding us good, and I ain talking chicken feed alone. Thing from the garden and thing."

A dog barked on a terrace below.

"Farmerman coming soon, you know."

"Now?" Rupert exclaimed.

"Morning and afternoon these days," Poncho informed them. "If the dog smell you, is trouble. You forget how you butt the farmerman by the woodpile, knock him down?"

"I ain forget," Rupert said.

"Farmerman ain forget either. You best go for true," Poncho pleaded. "He does walk with a gun these days. If he see you and can't catch you, he might look to kill me instead."

"He go do that anyway," Rupert argued.

"Maybe not," Poncho smirked. "See over there, back of that mess?"

Behind the rusted wheelbarrow was a gap where a piece of board had rotted away.

"If I want, I could get out," Poncho assured them. "But the hen them go soon be laying and chicks running all over the place. For true. The farmerman even might let me out if he see how . . ."

Poncho's words were cut off by the sound of footsteps approaching. Quickly, he flapped back to the hens and played at courting them. Rupert eased off the tire and into the tall grass; Viggo moved from the crate and slipped into one of the cans until only his head showed. Through a split in the planks, he could see a figure moving along the path to the coop. When the figure stopped at the coop door, Viggo heard the latch and the dreaded sound of what he couldn't see—a panting dog.

The door swung open, and Viggo saw a thick red-faced fellow dressed in brown overalls. He crossed the coop in a wide arm-swinging stride, all business, and sat on a crate. Then he pulled a file from his pocket and began sharpening the already gleaming blade of his machete. In rhythm to the grating file he sang a song. He hummed most of the verses because he didn't appear to know the words. But he never missed the refrain:

Times so hard
M'dog and all got to work.

After he finished this little ditty and the blade of his machete shone, he raised a malevolent eye at Poncho.

"So, Mr. Fowl-cock, any good news to report today?"

Poncho preened his feathers and pretended not to notice the farmer was addressing him. The hens continued their gentle clucking.

"Because I was thinking," the farmer went on, pocketing his file. "Last night, m'cousin tell me he got couple rooster up there chasing the hen them so bad they can't self rest." Here he paused and spat as if expecting his rooster to account for himself. Through the silence, Viggo caught a glimpse of the dog on the far side of the coop. Only the stench of the place and the direction of the wind was preventing the cur from picking up their scent.

The farmer lifted the hens up one at a time and pondered

the empty nests. He took off his straw hat and smoothed back his greasy hair, his tongue wandering in his cheek. Then he turned to Poncho and raised the machete's point level with the rooster's eyes.

"Fowl-cock," he said, "used to be you was the best fowl in the coop. Soon you go be the tastiest in the soup." He smiled at his rhyme and winked at Poncho, and Viggo saw past two tombstone teeth into the dark abyss of the farmer's mouth.

That sight and the sound of the dog scratching on the door served up the thought of his own body torn open on the green grass, his life running out of him. Uneasily, he shifted his weight in the can. For a second, the can teetered. He tried to bring it back and did, but suddenly something else bottomed out and the silent coop detonated into a crescendo of crashing cans.

"*What is this?*" the farmer bellowed above the explosion. "*Blasted ramgoat, I see you! I see you! And you ain go get away this time!*"

Viggo and Rupert shot through the grass and bolted up the cliff, sending a landslide of dirt behind them. From the road they looked back and saw the farmer climb into his jeep, his dog beside him. The engine roared alive, and the jeep jolted forward, spinning wild plumes of dirt into the air.

Rupert bounded down the road and at the first bend leaped off the edge and crashed through the bush. He stopped in the middle of it, with Viggo beside him, and craned his neck to listen.

The jeep wound west on the road above them.

"Gone," Viggo said with a sigh.

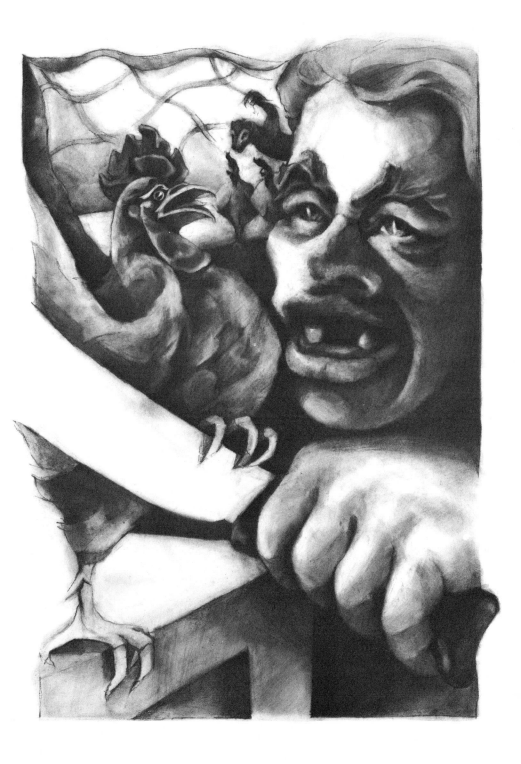

"Not for long," Rupert replied. "He go soon see we ain on the road, and he go turn back. Then is the gun or the dog."

"I sorry about the can them falling," Viggo said.

"You?" Rupert replied. "Is me suppose to be sorry. Poncho with he cock-foolery. But we ain got time for that. I know a goat trail down from here does go all the way mailbox tree and Bordeaux trail."

"To the bush?"

"To the bush."

"Come let's go then."

"But the farmer know the trail too," Rupert explained. "He done chase goat on it plenty time already. But it go soon be dark, and he ain go want to chop no bush at night."

Rupert stopped talking and turned his head to listen. At first Viggo heard only wind in the trees, but then another sound rose out of it—the stalling and stopping and idling persistence of an engine searching something out.

"Come quick," Rupert said in a whisper. Viggo followed him, heading deeper into the shadows.

The bush they were moving through was different from the forests Viggo had seen higher on the mountain. Here the green was a wild tangle of cow-tongue, casha, monkey puzzle, and cactus. It reminded him of his bush imaginings in the gut with Orville. Through the snarled tendrils he could make out the blue of the ocean, closer now than it had been from the road; he wished they could stop to listen and to see the blue move.

Soon, the bush opened onto the trail.

"This is it," Rupert said.

"The way to the bush?"

"Yes. But we ain go reach mailbox tree tonight. I got a friend on the trail we could stay with. We go be safe there long as the farmerman don't catch up."

"A next chicken coop?" Viggo asked.

"No, this more like a cave," Rupert explained.

"And your friend living there?"

"A good reliable fellow."

Viggo wondered if Rupert had considered Poncho equally good and reliable.

"What kind of fellow?"

"A big old iguana," Rupert replied.

"Oh, one of them," Viggo said with a brave smile, his insides aflutter at the prospect of a reptilian encounter.

Spike

Toward dusk Viggo sensed they were approaching the iguana's lair from a dense patch of razor-toothed ping-wing that surrounded an outcropping of huge boulders. Rupert led him onto a narrow avenue of dirt that snaked through the plants' treacherous arms and emptied on a dirt slope where great blue boulders jutted into the sky. Between them were slices of darkness, tunnels lacing through the stone.

Rupert leaped from one boulder to another and came

to a slab covered with lichen. He stared into one of the black spaces.

"Look like no one home," Viggo said, a note of optimism in his voice.

"He in there, though," Rupert assured him. "But he shy."

He stamped his hooves and gave a low baa. Then, in a tight black wedge between blue boulders, two silver half-moons appeared. The iguana's eyes.

"Hi, Spike," Rupert said cheerfully.

Pebbles rolled out of the cave mouth and a gray-green head emerged, turned sideways, and surveyed them. The eye was encircled by wrinkles, the mouth parted like a scaled beak. A comb of leathery blades sprouted from the head like swords testing the sky. This, Viggo realized with a touch of contentment, was a real beast—more than Prosper's imaginings, more perhaps than what his ancestors had known. Truly, Rupert was leading him where he wanted to go.

A distant shock of lightning illuminated the eastern sky, and a low grumble of thunder rumbled behind. The eye rotated and a guttural rasp issued from the iguana's mouth.

"He don't sound very friendly," Viggo noted.

Now the iguana came entirely out on the ledge. He had a brilliant green body, a long sweeping tail, and blades like armor growing out of him.

"It got a storm coming, big fellow?" Rupert asked.

The reptile's eyes blinked twice. Out of a rasp grew a growl:

East wind, sky wide,
Squall up Anegada side.

Rockstone loose, jawbone tight,
Best stay here, rain tonight.

"He don't say much," Viggo observed, "but what he say sure sound sweet."

Rupert looked east at the weather. Clouds were moving in, and the sky was drawing over them like a shroud. Wisps coursed through the mountain passes, and mist roiled up from the valley floor. To the east, thunderheads towered over the smaller islands, billowing blue-gray and heading their way. Spike backed into a dark tunnel until only his head showed. Drizzle began to fall.

Rupert led Viggo through two vaults of stone to a third chamber that was dark but dry. In a storm it was a good place to be, but in the blackness, with their backs to the wall, it smelled to Viggo like a trap. Fresh bolts of lightning punctuated the gloom, and a cannonade of thunder, like huge wooden wheels, rolled westward.

As the sound receded, Viggo strained to listen.

"You hear that?" he asked Rupert.

"You think I deaf?" Rupert replied.

"Not the thunder. Listen."

There was an engine on the road above. The sound faded, picked up, then stopped.

"I hear it," Rupert said.

They went to the outer chamber to hear better and saw car lights fan through the high limbs. Their eyes locked. Out of a stone tunnel slithered the iguana, heading deeper into the cliff.

"If they go over the west side, we go get cut off," Rupert

said, his features drawn and serious. "And if they go east, the dog sure to pick up the scent and track us down. Unless it rain hard, wash away the scent."

The thwack of machetes echoed through the bush above their stone vault. Two men were working toward the cliff's edge.

"Hold still," Viggo said. Standing beneath Rupert's neck, he applied his teeth and claws to the rope that held the bell.

"What you doing?"

"I go use the bell to draw them off."

"No, Viggo," Rupert said, pulling away.

"I could outrun them," Viggo insisted.

Suddenly the machetes stopped, and the dog's barking turned into a howl.

"They find the trail," Rupert announced, his voice flat, his eyes bottomless, far back in his head.

Viggo continued working on the knot.

"Whatever happen," Rupert said, resigned to Viggo's efforts, "the trail go take you to the mailbox tree. The trail to Bordeaux. . . ."

"I go see you there in the morning," Viggo said, freeing the knot.

"Go east," Rupert instructed him. "Go to the gut we pass before and follow it down. Don't come back to the trail no matter what you hear, no matter what happen. And if you don't see me at the mailbox tree . . ."

"Wait for me there," Viggo said, not wanting to hear the rest. He took a last look at his friend. A flash of lightning made a halo of mist around Rupert's head.

♦

With the cord between his teeth, Viggo dragged the bell down the winding path, following its trickle of water until it emptied onto the main trail. Rolls of thunder played in the distance, and Viggo wished for the first time that the rain would flood down on them, that lightning would tear into the night. Perhaps then the men would go home.

The beams from two lights told Viggo where they were, just about to stumble on the path to the cliffs. Carefully, he crossed the trail and found a clearing on the east slope with enough space to run in. Beyond the clearing was a gut, strewn with boulders, turning its way down the hill. He heard the happy panting of the dog and knew his own scent had probably given him away. Then he heard the men.

"Eh eh!" one voice exclaimed. "Watch how he sniffing now. Look like he find something. Watch now, see how . . . *Look!* Some cave!"

A sudden bolt of lightning sizzled into the limbs above them, and a deafening crack of thunder raised a yelp from the dog.

"Geez!" a voice shuddered. "Like the sky taking aim, man." It was the farmer's voice.

Viggo could see them clearly now. The farmer was behind, holding a shotgun and shining a light on the trail. A taller, thinner man was in front holding a machete in one hand and the leash and a flashlight in the other. They were starting up to the caves, where they were sure to pick up Rupert's scent. Viggo had wanted to wait longer, but his time had come.

He bolted across the clearing, trailing the bell over the stones.

Clam bang-ga-lang dang, the bell sounded.

BRATAM! A shot rang out.

A hole ripped through the bush above Viggo, and shreds of leaf rained down.

"Over there!" a voice called out.

BRATAM!

BRATAM!

Something seared into Viggo's flesh, and he fell. He bit into the cord near the bell and, with a yank of his neck, flipped it over his head and into the gut. The bell banged onto the rocks, from boulder to boulder, drawing fire.

BRATAM!

BRATAM!

BRATAM!

Shots caromed off boulders and ripped through the green. The stench of gunsmoke filled the air.

The shots stopped. Viggo could see them—two flash-lights and a panting dog between them like an idling car. Low voices went back and forth and then quieted. Their lights started toward him. Viggo slinked into the gut, drag-ging a hind leg, and drew into a hollow of stone, the scent of his own blood heavy around him.

He heard them advance until he could feel them atop the very boulder he was hiding beneath. Blades of light played down the gut and pried between the stones looking for the beast who wore the bell. Viggo heard the eager panting of the dog, felt the metallic heat of the gun barrel passing through the stone.

"You think you hit him?" a voice asked.

"I believe we would have hear the goat bawl out," another replied.

Then Viggo caught the promising sound of a downpour closing in from the east. He listened to it, fearing the shower might miss them. Staring out at the drizzle, Viggo wished and waited.

Suddenly the rain began to fall in sheets, and just as quickly the flashlights lost interest in the boulders. Viggo heard words, some laughter, and a final guffaw. Now, he guessed, their fun was over. It was dark, and pouring, and there was probably saltfish and dumplings waiting in a pot at home.

Over the sound of the rain Viggo heard them clamber up the slope and into the jeep. Twin beams shot into the night sky, making tunnels of rain. The engine turned over, and the tunnels panned the darkness in reverse. Then the lights faded from sight.

Viggo touched his hind leg. Where had the pain gone? For a moment he fancied he'd imagined his wound. But the scent was unmistakable and the sticky wetness not like rain. A faint glimmer of lightning revealed the slick coat of red he wore from his thigh to his toes.

The sight of the wound wearied him. His body slumped back into a puddle, and water washed over him. He looked out at the sky and thought he saw a star, but his head rolled into the water and the star went black. His mother's face rose out of the darkness and shone down on him. Then he saw Manteoba and other faces—faster and faster, flickering past in the night. The water continued to rise and close around him, and he couldn't feel what he had been feeling, or taste the blood in the water, or hear the water that ran into his ear.

What the Wave Said

When the last cloud drifted west and the wind had died and the moon had risen over the bush, a frog continued to croak about his good fortune. A sodden lump of fur and bones had formed a dam in the gut so that even now, hours after the storm, there was still puddle enough to wallow in. But perhaps he shouldn't have thumped on the dam so hard or croaked so loudly, because the dam suddenly lifted and shook, and the frog's puddle drained away.

Viggo looked about, his heart pounding inside him, and remembered where he was. How much time has passed? he wondered. He looked at his leg in the moonlight; rainwater had washed the blood away and left three clean puncture wounds. He set to work with his teeth and paws, and after a few painful efforts he worked loose three tiny balls of lead. He washed his wounds again and rested.

For a while he stared through the darkness, alone and inside himself. Below him the boulders were webbed in moonlight, and through the trees he could see the ocean and the moon shining silver on the water. The hollow echo of waves pounding the shore brought to mind something Rupert told him, and he tested his leg, knowing where he wanted it to carry him. The boulders and the sound of water finding its way through them drew him down, stone by stone, closer and closer to the shore. He followed the gut's twists until they delivered him, finally, to a high perch overlooking the sea. He was in a well of stone with sheer cliffs to either side.

He edged up to the abyss, testing the brink with his toes, as if his weight alone could topple it. Below, a wave surged up and fell away, leaving a seascape of tortured faces etched in the cliff. The cliff frightened him, and so did his tiny place in things. He anchored himself into a stone socket and grew smaller still. He watched the liquid grace of a gathering wave and saw the lip unwind in a burst of spray, like a final exhausted sigh. Then some wisp of memory drew him out and led him down a new trail of thought. He followed it.

"I suppose to think something," he said to himself, as if he had learned once that this was what cliffs were for.

Instead, he thought about waves. He tried to imagine what it would be like rolling over all that deep, and how it would feel to finally wash ashore. Then he wondered how it would feel to miss the shore, to hit no island at all, and to roll never cresting through the night. He rolled with it, no longer thinking about what to think.

He drifted off, and from somewhere inside him a sigh escaped. The sea answered him over and over with the same message, surging through the cliff, and Viggo was falling away, between places, no place at all. The sea was in the cliff, and the cliff was humming a kind of tune the sea had heard before. But it was new to Viggo, and it curled up around him, and what it said put him to sleep . . .

The Mailbox Tree

The mailbox tree grew on the westernmost bend of Crown Mountain Road. Its trunk was wide, its limbs low and laden with mailboxes. Many of the boxes were old coffee cans or biscuit tins nailed to the tree, and sometimes the nails were a problem and the boxes a mixed blessing. But the tree had grown to accept them and to enjoy the comings and goings of people who put things in and took things away.

Behind the tree lay a path, an overgrown, mostly forgotten way, once known to the tree as an old plantation trail. Now few wandered down it because the main road had come to keep people from straying.

This was the way of roads, and the tree understood it because it had been with the road so long. Its roots grew under the road and helped hold it up so that the road could feed water to the tree and bring people to their boxes. The road and the tree were partners whose main activity was waiting.

The morning after the storm the tree waited, weary after a night of wind and rain. One old mailbox—flag rusted up, lid sprung like a tongue hanging down—seemed to say it best. But the tree's day held promise. The road still glistened with runoff, and its roots continued to drink. At sunup, a bright crew of parrots had taken a low swoop among its limbs and headed west. Now birds talked in the tree's top, and several mongooses skylarked in its roots.

Shortly after dawn the tree felt the familiar clipped trot

of a goat on the slope below. It measured the steps and felt the trail cough up a ram. The tree knew the goat and wondered where the old man was who usually walked with him. The tree looked at the road and wondered why, but the road didn't know. Nor did the field. And if the trail knew, it wouldn't tell.

The goat looked up and down the road and turned two circles in the dirt, sniffing the air. Then he went to the tree and settled into a cradle of roots where he'd waited before. Again the road was empty. One of the birds, then the others, left their limbs and swept down the mountainside, and the tree was alone with the goat.

The early cry of a gull woke Viggo at first light, stunning him with the enormity of the cliff, the shear stone face falling to the swirling sea. His perch seemed higher and more frightening than it had in the moonlight, and he backed away from it. He felt as if he were staring out of himself without really being inside, as if he could reach out and tilt the horizon to either side. In his head was the lilting memory of a sea song. Slowly, he started up the fallen flow of stone, noticing as he climbed that the boulders seemed less jumbled than before. A kind of harmony seemed to have befallen them, as if each stone had been carefully set in place.

Where the gut crossed the trail, Viggo stopped to sniff around the caves and visit the scene of the night before. Then he started west toward the mailbox tree to find Rupert. He quickly gathered speed, with each leap losing his shadow and regaining it. The trail torqued and straightened, dipped and climbed, and Viggo bound with it, as if he'd run the trail before, each foot knowing blindly where the next would land. Soon the trail wrapped south and west along a new ridge, then up to meet the road. The last of it was a steep stairway of root and stone. Viggo stopped halfway, long enough for his heart to catch up, and, on a warm rock, smelled a fresh scent very similar to his own. He looked around and in the deep silence and dappled light felt for an instant the passing feeling he'd felt before, the feeling of an unseen hand where root and rock and wind and tree—and even he, Viggo—were one.

Above him light showed on the slope where the road broke in on the green. He climbed the last of it and rose over the shoulder. The road he saw was unfettered by fence or wire, the bush crowding it on both sides. On a windswept rise overlooking the road stood the mailbox tree looking wizened and twisted and very much like its name. He saw in its roots a familiar shape and gave the last stretch his best burst of speed.

"Viggo!" Rupert shouted.

"Rupert!" Viggo exclaimed through a mustache of dust.

"I here worrying all the time," Rupert said, his hooves stamping the earth. "So *tell* me. Tell me all what happen."

So Viggo told him everything in his best storytelling way, making certain not to spare the panting dog or the smoking gun or the deadly wound. He parted the hair on his leg and bared the flesh where the pellets had entered.

"Eh eh!" Rupert exclaimed. "It don't hurt?"

"Only at first," Viggo said, brushing it off, standing bravely on his hind legs. Rupert looked him up and down.

"And then the farmer turn off?" he asked.

"I hear the motor gone."

"That was some shot, eh?" Rupert said, transported.

"But you ain hear the best," Viggo said.

The goat looked at him, trying to imagine what could be better.

"I went by the sea."

"By the sea?" Rupert's eyebrows raised.

"And a strange thing happen."

Rupert grew serious. "What kind of thing?"

"After the rain finish, I find a place with sea and cliff together. It had two big rockstone, and I sit down staring out."

"At the sea," Rupert said.

"And the star. And I stay there late until when the moon pass straight over my head and the sea turn silver and the wave them come up on the stone."

Here Viggo stopped, eyes wide, as if the story was over, as if it were enough that the moon should rise and the sea should be.

"But then what happen?" Rupert asked.

"And then," Viggo whispered, "I hear what the wave say."

"You hear it!" Rupert exclaimed. "What it was, man? What it say?"

Viggo searched back in his head.

"I don't remember," he confessed.

"You . . . you don't *remember*!" Rupert blasted.

"It wasn't word," Viggo tried to explain. "It pass through me. Through and through, deep and deep . . ."

Rupert nodded gravely.

"And it pass out going so," Viggo said, pointing over his shoulder to where the feelings had gone. Rupert followed Viggo's gesture to a green mailbox, half expecting the wave's words to roll out.

"It pass through you?" he asked Viggo.

Viggo nodded. "But I think I still have some inside."

"Inside," Rupert said in a ramgoat trance.

Silence returned to the tree and settled around them. Rupert rose and motioned Viggo to a rise of dirt where they could see west over the bending grass. Beyond lay the land of a long-ago story, hills of green like waves rolling to the sea.

"That is bush," Viggo murmured.

"Pure bush," Rupert replied.

Viggo looked out at it and wondered about something Clovis once said—that when he was truly in the bush, he wouldn't know it, he'd have even forgotten he was trying to get there. He wondered if perhaps he already had some bush inside.

"Had couple of mongoose playing around here," Rupert told him. "Just a short while ago."

"For true?"

"For true. Come, you see." He led Viggo to their tracks. The prints were small and fresh and hopscotched from side to side—little ones at play.

"If you go quick, you could catch up with them," Rupert encouraged him.

"Without you?"

"I go soon come," Rupert answered. "But let me stay here wait till the coalman come. You go make mongoose friend easier without me anyway."

"When I go see you?"

"You go soon see me," Rupert assured him. "All the mongoose them know where the coalman live because it underneath the mango tree."

"Oh," Viggo said, not thinking. Voices were coursing around inside him, real voices, ones he remembered. One voice, distant and small, he recognized as his own as it was when he was little and a dreamer on the churchyard wall. He looked back at the road twisting east like a ribbon and knew that far enough back on it there were faces and places still where they were before. Was this now to be lost, surrendered to the bush?

"Rupert?"

"What, Viggo?"

"When I go into the bush, I go forget I was looking to go there?"

"In a way it go wash through you, yes," Rupert replied.

Viggo looked again at the ribbon.

"You does forget everything?"

"Everything like what?"

"All like your friend them and where you was," Viggo explained.

"No, Viggo," Rupert said, shaking his head. "You ain never go forget that."

Viggo turned and looked at the bush—wild and green and waiting.

"It all downhill from here," Rupert said, looking over Viggo's shoulder. "This your moment, Viggo. Don't leave it pass you up."

"I go see you in the valley, then," Viggo said.

"In the valley, then," Rupert replied.

Viggo made off in a trot, turning to look back only once. Then wind gusted the treetops and the trail dipped and the bush took him in. The guinea grass rustled green and gold, and the shoots parted in the wind before him, and there was a sweet scent of mongoose in the air.